After 45 years of mundane employment, James Tully retired and took a holiday he had denied himself for many years. Upon travelling on a cruise ship which brought him to the Arctic Circle, he watched the blue sea pass before him and wrote the first draft of his first novel. He then spent six months rewriting the effort of those two weeks, mostly for the purpose of correcting spelling and punctuation.

Dedicated to all those who told me their stories, out of sheer boredom and then refused to listen to mine.

James Tully

# MUSIC MURDER

AUSTIN MACAULEY PUBLISHERS
LONDON * CAMBRIDGE * NEW YORK * SHARJAH

Copyright © James Tully 2024

The right of James Tully to be identified as author of this work has been asserted by the author in accordance with sections 77 and 78 of the Copyright, Designs and Patents Act 1988.

All rights reserved. No part of this publication may be reproduced, stored in a retrieval system, or transmitted in any form or by any means, electronic, mechanical, photocopying, recording, or otherwise, without the prior permission of the publishers.

Any person who commits any unauthorised act in relation to this publication may be liable to criminal prosecution and civil claims for damages.

This is a work of fiction. Names, characters, businesses, places, events, locales, and incidents are either the products of the author's imagination or used in a fictitious manner. Any resemblance to actual persons, living or dead, or actual events is purely coincidental.

A CIP catalogue record for this title is available from the British Library.

ISBN 9781035860524 (Paperback)
ISBN 9781035860531 (ePub e-book)

www.austinmacauley.com

First Published 2024
Austin Macauley Publishers Ltd®
1 Canada Square
Canary Wharf
London
E14 5AA

# Chapter One

Janney got off the bus and was feeling good. She had finished a two-week working assignment or maybe it was a working holiday. She didn't care what it was called; for the most part, she had not been spending her own money.

She left the UK just after Christmas 1965 and returned weeks later in the new year of 1966. She visited Paris, Amsterdam and Munich, travelled at the company's expense, attended concerts, often with backstage passes, spoke with musicians, promoters and agents and made contacts. She saw which venues worked and why, who she might contact again, maybe trust, but most importantly a partial view of how the British music scene was being exported, as well as presented, all for European consumption.

Europe had been an eye-opener she could not have anticipated. So much was new and unexpected. She had still yet to fully appreciate the different humour of the people she met. German humour had both delighted and confused her.

She had a folder, which she hoped was a meticulous report. She knew she would never stop rewriting any of the work she started. The graduates she dealt with seemed to enjoy correcting her written and spoken grammar, always smiling to her face and nearly always within earshot of others.

Her memory was clear, the times they watched her, waiting for the reaction, all the times she remained as still as she could, doing her best to stay employed.

When she left school, it was with a desperate hope to get away from the housing estate flat she shared with her mother. She left home with no clear plan for what she wanted; she didn't know if it could ever be found.

Now it seemed at last she had a chance for a life, a good life. She was an assistant to one of the head managers of Artist Development, within one of the largest music recording and music publishing companies in the UK.

Janney walked down the office corridors to reach her desk, which in truth she hardly ever used. She passed a room full of typists, the place she first worked when she came to MCM Plc only five years earlier.

She gave out the obligatory "Mornin', mornin'" to anyone who looked towards her with a greeting. One girl with a cut-glass accent looked up with her usual disdain.

Janney recently discovered that 'Deborah'—she always insisted everyone pronounce each vowel—was incensed Janney could carry off such an upfront unselfconscious attitude, speak with a 'rough' working-class style, whenever she met the bosses or whenever speaking with her for that matter and yet still seem casual in polite company. "Mornin," said Janney as she passed by Deborah, stressing all the consonants. Janney kept any form of anger deep within herself; it was hers; no one else's business.

One day Janney fell upon a belief she then held tightly onto, showing anger was humiliating. She instinctively felt 'Anyone able to force your anger will take you away from yourself, they can drive a route into your own sense of self.'

To those around her, if there was ever anger beneath Janney's easy-going public exterior, it would never show itself, except on a rare occasion, then only in her eyes.

Part of Janney's private world was that since leaving school, leaving home, she had become more and more self-conscious of how she spoke, her accent, of any errors in her spoken grammar, her overall lack of education.

She recalled times, her confidence, her sense of self-worth would vanish, just disappear. She could be consumed by strong anxiety. A retreat then to a quiet place, moments of cold fury, brought her back towards feeling safe.

For years, Janney had been marking time, just improving her typing speed. One day her luck changed in a way she never dreamt.

A senior manager, Malcolm Offen, announced there was to be a restructuring of the staff within his division. He gave out tasks to secretaries, administrative staff, paralegals, even messengers, tasks no one expected from researching news items, making lists of addresses and sometimes, just making tea. Then everyone had to report back to him.

No one was quite sure what he was after, but after a while, it was clear he had noticed and paid attention to the thoughts and behaviour of some staff more than others.

Janney spotted Derek Ball over by the filing cabinets, picking away at drawers. He saw her enter. She saw his big welcoming smile.

Janney liked Derek. He was a great conversationalist and seemed to have something to say on every given subject. Unlike others she met within the organisation, he wanted to share any useful things he discovered with everybody. He tried to make all he learnt sound interesting for others.

Derek was 22, which gave Janney at 26, a feeling of definite seniority. Derek was an administrative linchpin. He knew where record sales changed following tours or if a television appearance boosted sales.

He had a great talent for keeping track of money. He and Janney had both been plucked out of obscurity by Malcolm Offen. Neither was aware of whatever they had done that had seemed so right.

Derek came across the room. "Great that you're back. How was cafe society? Have you learnt how to smoke those French cigarettes out of the side of your mouth, as well as talk and eat at the same time?"

Janney laughed; Derek seemed to have no ill will towards anyone.

Of course, this was irrelevant to people who never tried to know him but still took a moment from their day to call him offensive.

Derek walked with Janney between the desks. "Malcolm wants you in his office as soon as you have your coat off. No worries, I don't think it's anything urgent."

Janney and Derek were both within listening distance of Deborah. Each was aware of the new unofficial demarcations in status that had been recently set up for those sitting at desks. Janney could never resist rubbing noses in it.

"Ta Derek. Got a lot to report. One big advantage abroad, they never noticed the way I spoke. As far as they knew, I might 'ave been speaking the same way as the Queen Mother." Janney waved goodbye with both hands to everyone as she walked between the chairs, making it clear she was on her way to see the boss while they were still stuck behind their desks.

## Chapter Two

Malcolm Offen had a small office, three small cabinets, and four telephones. He spent much of his day either on the telephone, dictating letters into a recording machine or drawing out action plans in a very large notebook.

People had become aware that Malcolm seemed never to examine documents, relying instead on others to explain them. After meetings with managers, agents, promoters or lawyers, he might then privately read through the documents. If the papers contained what he regarded as salient points or issues and these had not been raised voluntarily by others, then those same others would depreciate in his estimation and trust.

Malcolm Offen knew his orders would always be followed. He was more impressed with those who would tell him what he did not know, or better still, what he needed to know, especially when someone told him he was in error.

Malcolm Offen left the army in 1945. He then left everyone he knew, family and friends, and went to America. He called on family connections to get him a position within a music company in New York.

His job, which he came to love, was to visit all the clubs in the city, to seek out new talent, often upcoming jazz artists, then if it all seemed to be a good idea, offer a record deal.

These deals offered little more than an opportunity to record and a chance to be heard on local radio. If the record was not an immediate success, the contract would expire.

Jazz artists were predominately black, they never expected much from the records they made. Many were paid a flat fee, often without a royalty rate for any record sold. No way to learn if sales were ever large or if royalties became owed.

As time went by it was apparent that everyone was making money from the records except the performers. If it was brought to their attention, they just shrugged their shoulders and said, "What else is new?"

If the record was played on the radio and became popular, the artist or combo might get more work in the clubs, better agents, better fees. Record-making could be a decent piece of work for a day or so, but it was not particularly exciting.

Malcolm had an appreciation for jazz that a lot of his colleagues at the company failed to even try to acquire. Malcolm was in the right place and at the right time to latch onto a changing jazz and doo-wop scene.

The development of bebop and street harmony groups, as well as emerging specialist radio stations, developed new markets no one saw coming.

By the time 'cool jazz' and television kicked in, Malcolm found himself one of the few executives able to respond to the rapid changes.

Malcolm signed some of the first rock and roll artists, but he had no interest in the music. For reasons he never discussed with anyone, he eventually returned to the United Kingdom. In late 1956, he stepped back onto UK soil for the first time in 11 years.

Janney spotted Malcolm looking down on his graphs and lists of numbers and she would have had no idea what any of them meant. She carried a lot of loyalty towards Malcolm. He had taken her from a job she thought she would be stuck in for years. With hindsight she knew it was the sort of work, at that time, she would have even been satisfied to stay in, expected to have to stay in, perhaps for years. The world was not as broad and wide at 21 as it was now at 26.

"Did you have a good time?" Malcolm asked without looking up, just as Janney entered.

Janney sat down and placed her paperwork and folder on the floor by her side.

"There is a lot going on over there, that's for sure."

"Not as much as when I was your age."

"You should see the folk clubs in Paris—very different from here. You should see the people they get in them. Some clubs allow poets to perform, they went down well."

Malcolm sat back. He always enjoyed Janney's company. "They have always been like that. French music is unique to France. The language I suppose, especially that Chanson stuff. You can always spot a French song, even after it's translated into something else."

"Chanson realiste, to be precise," corrected Janney, pleased with herself that she picked up the full phrase and could say it correctly. "The French sing as if they already expected your attention. It would have helped if I spoke French. You don't cross the channel much, do ya?"

"I can get by without it. Saw Paris again once I came back to England. It looked very strange to me, as if the war never happened."

Janney thought it better to get off the subject. She knew Malcolm had what some people called 'a bad war.' She had seen his eyes shift whenever the subject was raised. Better to talk about something else.

Malcolm had signed up at 21 straight out of university, as soon as the first bombs fell. With his degree and because his family knew how, he found himself to be a junior officer.

He started his military life joking with ordinary servicemen about his previous escapades as a student at university. He had no idea how this made the men view him.

One day the senior officers pulled him aside and gave him some strong advice he eventually came to understand, increasingly more so as the war progressed.

After the war, he returned home and a few months later left for America. He said he never again wanted to see any serviceman, anyone who had risked his life, asking for a job, holding their hand out, or having to say 'please' to people who stood in silence waiting to hear it.

Malcolm jumped out from behind his desk.

"Let me get us a coffee. Yours is milk, no sugar, right?" Malcolm went to a side table where there was a kettle with three big white mugs and an unopened silver-top bottle of milk.

"As I discussed briefly with you before you left, we have a few problems. What they are essentially depends on your viewpoint. In any event, with your help I intend to identify the important issues and we then can decide what to do."

Janney saw Malcolm was about to slip into his usual 'take charge' mode of instruction.

Malcolm brought the coffee back to his desk. Malcolm was taking a breath to set himself up for one of his staccato speeches where he hammered out bullet points for everyone around him to consider.

"Since the restructuring, we are now working with artist managers to help them send bands and singers on tours. Essentially, we now help managers book their clients into venues, contact the promoters, help put tours together, format contracts and whatnot. Believe me, they need a lot of help."

"Over the last few years, some bands have come back from touring with no money in their pockets, sometimes even owing money. They turn up at venues where there has been no promotion, halls half full, even with a record in the charts. Sometimes they are on the same bill with some other rubbish or inappropriate act which may have already attracted the wrong crowd anyway for our performers. It can all get very embarrassing."

Malcolm took a breath and began again "Some venues give inaccurate information on what's collected at the box office or of any money made through concessions. It's a money grab for a lot of them. Worst of all, some of the venues have a PA or a speaker system that's from the Stone Age. The records being made lately require a half-decent PA system for performance. Some bands travel with part of what they need but it can't continue to be taken for granted."

Malcolm then placed his finger on the desk. "The bottom line is that I am getting too many complaints and rightly so.

Some of our signed artists are talking about changing companies. They are starting to see their managers for what they are, amateurs, who just lucked into a new form of business."

"We must put bands in the right places and keep them happy, especially if we want them to stay on board. As well as give them a chance to keep producing the goods."

Janney felt she needed to interrupt this stream of consciousness coming her way if only to allow for a bit of consideration on what's been said, maybe give them both a chance to step back and focus on the words.

"Yer right. Yer absolutely right! I spoke to our signings while they were at clubs and halls on the continent. Some of them are amazed at the better sort of help and consideration they get when over there."

Janney picked up her folder and began to open it. "The acoustic and equipment problem, I think, is standard. Some studio sounds these days have become too advanced and detailed to reproduce in most concert halls, especially with the old speakers and equipment fitted into some of these small or medium-sized venues. Yer right about how embarrassing it can get. You should hear what they sound like when they haven't got the right amplification and mixing in place."

Malcolm sat back and seemed to relax, then smiled.

"Thanks, Janney, I knew I could rely on you. I want you to see what can be salvaged from any genuine efforts now being ruined through the greed of others. Especially the way the whole music scene is changing. It's getting hard to keep up with it. I want you to work with the different divisions in the office and collect details. I want you to form a real dialogue with all the departments, keep your eye on things."

"I also want you to be able to call on all of them and them on you, especially for information on two issues."

Malcolm sat back, taking a breath. The points were about to pour out again.

"I want to know which promoters, agents and venues to avoid, who is unhappy, where how and why the groups and singers are dissatisfied. You're going to get a lot of feedback on that. You're going to have to put up with a lot of unreasonable demands and stupid opinions, especially from their managers." Malcolm could not hide the contempt.

Malcolm looked for a reaction and saw none. "Make sure everyone knows you're the go-to girl. For both complaints and information. I am asking a lot here; the managers of these bands have a lot to protect. They want to be seen as being demanding, so their clients can stay impressed by their efforts. If managers begin acting up or start behaving like unreasonable idiots, do not be intimidated by that. It's more than likely they are idiots."

Malcolm gave time for a response, he began again. "Secondly, and you will have to work with Derek on this, the performers have expressed concerns how their money is organised. They need rehearsal rooms, studio time, transport and accommodation and they do not know what they are paying for, who is paying for what, or what any of it costs."

Malcolm knew he was doing all the talking, but saw that Janney was still staying on board. "They do not know where or how money is being put away for them, or where to even find it, or if expenses are being offset against taxes. People are finding out they owe taxes on money they have never seen. All of this is the tip of the iceberg. I want you to be the action point for people to ask their questions. Let them think you're always available, if you need an assistant, let me know. Report back to me anytime you have important information. Come and see me every Monday morning at 9am for a quick update on all that's happened in the week."

Janney felt it was now expected she could either speak up or just leave and get started, but she needed to grab his attention, make a few points of her own.

"There is some stuff I heard going on while I was over there, a lot was hard to understand, people didn't really want to talk. A lot of performers, mostly the American bands, are now asking venue managers, as well as promoters, really informed questions, questions about money. That by itself is fair enough but from what I kept hearing, there are unknown movers and shakers about, sowing discontent, giving out misinformation, trying to get people to change representations. Venue managers have started avoiding agents and promoters, after being told stories. Trust is being lost. People are getting angry and paranoid. It seems friendships, as well as businesses are being affected by rumours, often outright lies, all the way down the line. There have been a few stories of intimidation".

Malcolm stared at Janney for a moment. He eventually sighed, "Sounds like a 'power play.' I saw this sort of thing happen in America. Once a market changes and there is a chance for big money, especially if a lot of 'off the books', 'cash in hand', transactions are possible, these people, gangsters really, come out of the woodwork. They corner a piece of the market, pick away at all they can get. Once they dominate the weaker players, they take over, find the money flow, try and control the box office. Don't worry about this, Janney, if you hear more, let me know. I will make my own enquiries, this could be important, we will talk again once I know more. Make a list of names and contact details of people you spoke to, list any of those you think can be trusted and might be happy to take my call."

Janney slowly put her folder down by her side. "One other thing that has also started happening by itself is that bands are using rehearsal rooms for longer periods, to not just practice new material but to experiment with new electronic equipment, new sounds, different recording techniques. Finding ideas that might help them write new material. I have a feeling a lot of it is gonna be a waste of time and could become a black hole money-wise, but I think it's important to give leeway. These are creative people after all. It's possible a diamond can be pulled out of the toilet."

Malcolm thought for a few seconds and then laughed. "I suppose you're right. The days when a few guys rehearsed new material in an empty bar after hours are gone now."

Janney needed to press another point. "There are a few venues which have small mobile studios in their building, and bands are offered the use of these for free. A chance to experiment and record demos, by way of compensation for receiving a small fee for playing there."

Malcolm leaned back, clearly impressed. "I like the sound of that, a bit of initiative. Spread the word about those places. It might save some cost of renting out rehearsal rooms. Thanks for letting me know about that."

Malcolm smiled again. "Now on a separate note, will I see you at David's little soiree this Saturday?"

"Got the invitation. I will be there. It will be nice to meet some people I have only spoken to on the telephone."

"Oh, they will know who you are. Carry the invitation; there will be security at the door. You bringing a bloke?"

"No bloke."

"Well, see you then. Finish your report and leave it on my desk.

# Chapter Three

Janney left Malcolms office and closed the door. The open-plan scheme did not apply to him; neither did the 'My door is always open' motto that some managers seem to enjoy telling their staff.

She realised she had to think things through. There were a lot of new balls bouncing in the air. It would be easy to waste a lot of time. A plan of action was necessary. If only to slow her down and help organise her thoughts.

At a Christmas party, one of the older managers pulled her aside and gave some good advice, advice she decided to follow. *'The first thoughts to run through your head should only be that: the first thoughts.'*

He explained the danger of holding onto any first ideas and assumptions and then having all subsequent ideas and thoughts formed only to support those initial impressions.

Janney often thought hard over that conversation. She looked again at the mistakes she made in her life, often after making choices, decisions that were never even necessary.

She saw Derek making yet another cup of coffee. She pulled a chair over to Derek's desk.

"Looks like we might be working together."

Derek sipped his coffee. "Yes, I think Malcolm is trying to place you between him and all the nuisance calls. You may become the centre for all enquiries. The office guru!"

In the time Derek and Janney had known each other, She became aware that Derek carried an assumption everyone would always appreciate hearing his never-ending views, especially on what he called 'the real world.'

"You know whatever you say to these characters might never be good enough. Malcolm is the only person here the nutcases are polite to."

Janney suddenly saw a bit more method to the madness. "I will wait to see how things develop but the reality is beginning to dawn."

Derek stared into his coffee. "If you think about it, it makes sense. He had to delegate. He clearly trusts you. He must believe you're capable, oh! sorry, of course you're always capable!" Derek held both hands up.

"Listen, Janney, you must be careful now. This means a lot of work. You might have to delegate some yourself. There are a few people here who are jealous of you, so do not always assume promises will be kept. One other thing, a lot of singers and musicians are ready to imagine they are richer than they are, as well as very ready to say they have been cheated when they suddenly discover the well is running dry."

Derek leaned forward. Janney knew that Derek was always hovering close to exasperation. He hated being confronted with unreasonable behaviour, especially as he himself always wanted to be seen as honest and fair.

"I will give you details of where the money comes in and out, but if I tell you that tours are costing more than they are making, please pass that information on."

Derek made a sad face. "I don't want another idol of millions staring at me open-mouthed, ready to call me a thief, if I say he doesn't have money to buy a fancy car."

He saw Janney agreeing with him, but he also saw she was getting ready for matters to be all business.

"I might need to receive some quick, specific, information on how and where money is being spent. Can you act on that?"

Derek nodded. "I will do my best, but a lot of people coming through here feather their own nest. There are cash transactions on tours and at the concerts. Once people get cash in their paws, they develop a big sense of self-entitlement. They start to see it as all theirs!"

Janney smiled. "Enough said! Do not worry, I will not go around quoting you. Let's talk in the next few days. Will you be at David's party?"

Derek groaned. "Yes, but you're not going to believe this. Brian Nicholls cornered me and begged to be my plus one. For some reason, he is desperate to speak to Malcolm. He has been trying to get an appointment to see him since before Christmas. I had to say yes. The guy has done me a load of favours, ever since we were students together. I had a plus-one invite to a party full of pop stars, could you imagine what I could have done with that? Once the typing pool found out, I got waved at by girls who didn't care if I was alive a week ago."

"I keep telling you, Derek, just introducing a girl to a pop star will only get you so far. You would do as well if you just relaxed a little, desperate is not that attractive."

Janney nearly bit her tongue; the word was out before she heard it in her head.

"Sorry, man! I didn't mean that. It's just that you need to be choosier who you ask out. A lot of women are going to waste your time. Going to the party with Brian is not a bad thing, it will free you up to meet women at the party."

"Maybe", Derek smiled. "Brian can be my wingman, help me get a girl on her own if she comes with a friend."

"That's the spirit, there are women out there lucky to even know you. If you get the chance, try and push some Brian's way".

Janney remembered Brian Nicholls, Derek introduced him one night at the Back Door, a popular new venue. The 'Door' as it was known, was more like a converted large pub, with a high stage at the back. It had once been an old cinema in years gone by.

It was one of those places Janney had mentioned to Malcolm. It had a large basement that luckily retained a lot of working electrical points.

The owner had covered the basement walls with something to make it soundproof, at least in theory, then filled it with speakers, drums, keyboards and whatnot, plus a couple of reel-to-reel recording machines.

Before he knew it, he did not have to rent the space out. He had bands ringing him offering to play the stage, for a small fee, if they could just rehearse, experiment with new equipment and make demonstration tapes after hours.

Janney remembered Brian well. He appeared as an innocent sort of soul. She recalled he had an obvious habit of focusing very hard on whoever was speaking and then appearing quickly surprised at whatever had just been said.

Brian Nicholls was known at the office as an excellent musician, flute and keyboards. He had studied at a music college. He could write complete score arrangements. He found occasional on-call short notice session work in the studios, always happy to sit with any three or four-piece keyboard and wind combinations. Between session work he worked behind the bar at the Back Door.

Suddenly, they both realised someone was looming over them; then in the space between them.

In another situation, Derek would have said, "Excuse me but this is a private conversation."

The man was Johnny Lately. Derek stayed quiet, he had to remember they were all at work and this man was a client, as well as a visitor. Johnny Lately leaned into what was clearly uninvited space.

"Hello all! Did I hear you say you would be at David Offen's party this weekend?" Johnny Lately made an obvious point of speaking only to Janney.

Janney moved around in her chair to give him space. "Yes, that's correct, you have good hearing."

"Well, I will see you there. Excuse me again but did I also hear you both say that Brian Nicholls would be there?"

Derek turned his chair. He did not like being ignored and then hearing questions while looking behind a person's back, all about what had been his private conversation. He decided to get the man's attention.

"That's right, I am over here, I am the one who said that. Where do you know Brian and David from?"

Johnny slowly turned from Janney to Derek.

"Brian is my favourite bartender." There was a long pause. "David managed me for five minutes several years back, we are old friends." Derek turned back to Janney.

"Well, I will see you." There was an obvious pause, he turned sideways, "Both of you then. Bye." Johnny Lately walked away as if he had just won an argument.

Derek thought for a moment. "You know people accuse me of handing out labels, but that guy is a definition all by himself. There must be a word for what that guy is, I will have to study a thesaurus."

Janney said, "Forget him. Malcolm told me he is in the last dance saloon."

Johnny Lately had been one of a dozen or so overnight pop stars when rock and roll hit the UK in the late fifties. He could play a little guitar and he had written two songs, both of which barely broke the top twenty. He appeared two or three times on television, then disappeared.

Last year, one of his old songs was reintroduced on television as part of a successful car advertisement. *'My car can drive; it keeps me alive.'*

On the strength of this, he was allowed another record release. It was called 'Slipped Away,' which much to everyone's surprise was becoming a success.

Johnny Lately wrote the song. It had banal lyrics but there were independent musical runs on two different instruments, playing alongside with their own melody, against that of the guitar chords, changing and moving away from the songs initial tune. The record had everyone talking.

Much to everyone's chagrin, Mr Johnny Lately was now telling anyone who would listen he had a new album coming out.

Janney drank her coffee. "I would like to know who produced that record of his. Whoever it was has a future."

Derek rolled his eyes, "When that record was released, he came in every day. He wanted to know the record sales, the royalty payments, the money for the radio plays, and the rate he would receive should anyone else record the song."

"He kept insisting his name be on the copyrights, words, music, the arrangements. He wanted to see all the paperwork for confirmation."

Janney was surprised. "Really? He does not strike me as that clever."

Derek chuckled, "He is ready to do the same now for the album he has coming out. He has not even started recording it. He gives interviews in the music press where he mentions musical contemporaries. He quotes influences. He tells people he has been researching the blues."

Derek and Janney both laughed. Janney told a story of a folk club she used to visit, where one day some white teenager asked if he could play a few songs he found in an old blues catalogue. "Sure," said the landlady, herself a bit of a blues historian, "happy to hear it, if you can play it."

The poor guy sat on stage played his guitar and with his regional accent, started to sing a slave song from the previous century.

The landlady ran on stage and told him to stop and if he had no sense of what he was doing, there were a few people there willing to explain it to him.

Derek considered the point. "You know the rules on copyright are tricky, some old folk and blues songs have unknown authors. Bands claim an additional royalty rate after adding only a small extra arrangement, often just a few extra chords. who is going to challenge them."

Derek looked at the clock, "I have a lot to get on with, I will see you at David Offen's house this Saturday."

"See you then, I will keep quiet on the fact that you have already given up your plus one."

# Chapter Four

Janney spent the rest of the day saying, "Ello, Appy New Year," answering questions about Europe and passing off never-ending inquiries about her private life. When the day finished, she took the bus to visit her mother.

Janney sat on the bus and saw the architecture change as she moved across town. She left the bus and climbed the hill approaching the housing estate where she grew up. She was not religious, but she always said a silent '*Thank you*' when she saw the old estate and felt grateful, she had managed to get away. She remembered how it nearly broke her spirit. As a teenager, she had nowhere to compare it to; it seemed to be the whole world.

The aggressive movements from people that used to surround her as a young girl appeared no longer there, or maybe people were still the same but a little more polite. There was an appearance of more affluence. People seemed to have better clothes, better cars in the street.

Janney wondered whether buying better goods was just a new way for people to try and outdo their neighbours. Still, it was better than strutting around, arrogant faces, fighting in the streets. She was so glad to be away from it.

Some faces seemed happy. She knew her mother was happy. All the mini dramas that went on around her, seemed to pass right over the top of her head.

Janney's mother and father came over from Ireland in the 30s. Janney's mother, Irene, suffered a miscarriage with her first child and then with money and jobs scarce, they decided to wait before trying again.

Janney's father Ronald was from north of the British border and Irene came from 10 miles away, south of the new partition. Both were born as British subjects, just a few years before Ireland gained independence. Irene always joked she became Irish while Ronald remained British, he still belonged to the British Empire, still had to bow to the foreign king.

Ronald, being a British subject, was conscripted when the war began. Irene became pregnant after his first leave. Once he returned to his unit, she never saw him again.

Irene came running to the door when she heard Janney knock.

"Hello, hello, hello, come on in. You must tell me all about it. Did ya get to ride in an aeroplane?"

"No Mum. Got you a few gifts though." Janney sat down on the same settee she used to climb up upon when she was a child and opened her bag.

"Here is a scarf from Paris. These are large mittens all the way from Amsterdam. Help to keep your fingers warm in the winter. Is that little fridge I got you still working?"

"It is. The milk and butter last longer now. It saves money that way, but it still uses a lot of electricity. It's on all day and all night."

Irene had never lost any of her Irish accent, despite living two-thirds of her life in England.

Janney could hardly hear Irene's accent when she faced her mother, but she heard it clear as a bell when they spoke on the telephone.

"It doesn't really, Mum. I want you to have a look-see."

Janney took a melon out of her bag and some tubs of ice cream.

Irene had few interests or hobbies except her indoor plants and a desire to try all the new fruits which were now appearing for the first time in the new supermarkets, especially the different melons.

"Mum! These are new flavours of ice cream. When you're eating your melon, you first cut it in half and make a hole in the middle and drop some ice cream in the hole. Keep these tubs in the top of the fridge if they start to melt."

Irene sat back. "Gosh, you travel and getting around, I wish I could see it with you. I would have loved to see Notre Dame Cathedral. My school in Ireland was called Notre Dame. The Sisters of Mercy used to always talk about going there one day."

Irene read the labels on the ice cream. "I bet none of them ever stepped out of that bog hole of a town. Some of them were nice to me though. Sometimes, whenever they felt like it."

"Was it really as bad as that?"

"Aw, that's all over now. You should have seen the place I grew up in. The whole place was full of dug-up holes where the turf had been taken out by the farmers. The holes used to fill up when the rain came."

"I can still remember the mud and the smell of rainwater. I remember the smell of wet grass. I used to like that. The colours as well. You can't smell the grass here."

"So how are things? Got a boyfriend yet?"

"No boyfriend, Mum, let it be."

"You know you're an attractive girl. What's wrong with fellers around here? A lot of men these days look like girls with their long hair. Not just over their ears but now right down their back. You're still mixing with those pop stars?"

"Yeah, in fact, I am going to a big party this Saturday. There will be a lot of them there."

"Maybe you could nab yourself one of these fellers off the telly."

"Mum, I do not go out looking for men, ok! Anyway, the place will be full of models and whatnot."

"What the hell has that got to do with anything?"

"Well, they really hold onto their men, Mum."

Irene was silent for a moment. "You know, thieves," she paused, "believe everyone steals."

Janney raised her eyebrows in surprise. "Where did that come from?"

Irene sat down. "I am just saying, it's something to consider. It might be worth applying it to yourself."

"Mum, I do not go around stealing men."

"Oh! For goodness' sake, get on board, I didn't say that."

"I have watched you change these last few years. You're starting to believe you know now how every other person thinks, or that they must in some way think just like ya. A lot of people living around here have that same sort of attitude."

"You ever consider how many ideas you had that are stupid now when you remember them? You need to look at the person you're turning into. There is never a need to settle. Don't take the quick way out. Don't be like the nuns. Be yourself, be your whole self."

"I can't hold your hand anymore and tell you things are going to be ok. Find a way to let go of the past, or at least live with it. Try to trust people or allow for the differences between you and them. Be more open, open with yourself."

"Yes, Mum, I am getting better. I have a good job now. My boss thinks I am doing well."

"Why shouldn't he? Listen, if you meet someone who seems cleverer than you, well, good luck to them but often, that's just practice. There are all sorts of tricks to talking with people."

"You're right, Mum, I just go a bit quiet amongst educated people. I don't wanna interrupt if I have no idea what they are talking about."

"Some people use difficult words to try and make you think they understand difficult things. They talk of ideas they never use, Ideas they repeat from other conversations."

"Well, I can't tell the difference, Mum."

"Well, there is nothing wrong with that, just hold on to the space you're in and remember, you do not have to answer every question, if you do, take your time and make them all wait till you finish speaking."

"Don't try to compete with these women at the party either, you work for a living! You have your own games to play. Be careful of ever playing games with your friends. Watch for how all the days change."

Irene brightened "You know my father used to tell me that and I still have no idea what it means. We can spend all our lives remembering rubbish. Remember this! Your best friend is your pocket!"

"OK! Mum. OK! Let's change the subject. You must stop annoying yourself. You know, Mum, I am thinking of getting a car. Maybe I could take you to one of those bigger supermarkets outside town. Get some of the new melons."

"Make sure you get a driving licence first. Learn to drive."

"I will, Mum, do you want to try this melon and ice cream now?"

Irene was delighted with the melon. She suggested Janney should try and sell the idea of dipping the ice cream into the centre of the melons. Janney said she would try for a copyright. Irene told her to do that as well.

Janney and her mother found out together there was a big difference between ice cream and a new thing called sorbet. Janney had thought sorbet was another ice cream flavour.

Once they had cleaned up, they watched a variety show on the television. Janney pointed out the people she had met and knew.

Irene shook her head, "What amazes me is surely someone must have heard this crowd before they were allowed on the show. Whoever told him he was funny anyway. Look at those faces he pulls."

Janney promised her mother that the next time she met them she would tell a few of the acts that they should learn better jokes and maybe how to sing.

"Someone should have done them a favour a long time ago and put them straight." Irene showed the face which made it clear she had definite views.

Janney thought again of the differences she saw between the English and the Irish. The way Irish people would only laugh at what they genuinely thought was funny, even if others around them never saw the joke.

Janney and Irene talked for hours about Europe and the relatives Irene left in Ireland, the troubles that were going on in the northern counties. Irene said the seeds were planted there a long time ago.

"Some people will do anything to hold onto what they imagine they have. They get frightened of having their views challenged. Sometimes it might only be the idea that they are no different from others or not already born better than others. History ties these people down to what they think they ought to be. It's all just imaginary." Irene chuckled to herself.

Janney watched her mother and knew her mother had never needed to sell her opinion, or waste time to argue with anyone for what was right or wrong.

Janney left her mother when it was clear Irene wanted to get to bed and then she caught the night bus back to her flat. There was a lot to catch up with before Saturday.

# Chapter Five

David Offen's house was hidden behind trees and a high metal fence. It had a long driveway up to the house, which was going to be useful as a few cars would be attending that night. There was a winding path from the gate up to the house with security at the front door as well as the gate and fence. Several famous faces had already left cars in the driveway and on the lawn.

Some people were so 'obviously' cool they parked away from the house and approached the front gate on foot, hands in pockets. There were photographers and autograph hunters at the gate after all, a chance to show the common touch for the newspapers.

Despite David Offen's public 'man of the people' persona, his house, much to his own surprise, had become his pride and joy although he would never be so crass as to admit the same.

David suffered no delusions about the real benefits wealth and success had brought, as well as all the early perspectives it became possible to forget. Much as he was loath to admit it, in this new egalitarian age, in his heart he was happy to be exactly what everyone said he appeared to be.

The house was three stories high with an attic on top and had a very large back garden. Tables had been set out with food and two large punch bowls. There was a bar, in charge of which David had hired a 'mixologist', a woman who threw drinks into the air, all landing in a long glass. David had seen her behind the bar at a famous London hotel one night and booked her for the evening.

Malcolm and David were cousins and when apart no one would have seen the connection. David had long hair and a short beard which suited him. He even on occasion let metal hang around his throat.

Malcolm had short hair, wore conservative colours and despite this, always looked more stylish than his cousin.

When seen together the family resemblance was clear, especially when they both laughed simultaneously at some joke only the two shared.

David was 10 years younger than his cousin, had missed the war, but completed his National Service. He had no idea what healthy and fit really meant until he took his first deep breath while climbing on ropes halfway up a mountain. He remembered thinking, 'This is worth knowing.'

When Malcolm returned from America in 1956, he was quickly recruited to build a new department at MCM Plc, Record Sales Division, to sell the new rock and roll music.

David Offen was at a loss after National Service. He hated the idea of going to university. Malcome agreed with his family to guide his cousin into Artist Management. Malcolm put David in touch with people who could show him the ropes and give him work. David had found his calling in life.

David eventually left behind management and moved into arranging and promoting concerts and tours; Malcolm and

David cornered their little square inch of the market. Working together they became a force to be dealt with.

Malcolm watched the people entering, all the beautiful women holding coats over their arms. He caught sight of Johnny Lately arriving at the door, surprisingly he was alone. Malcolm quickly turned to David.

"What is he doing here?"

David sighed, "He contacted me and asked for an invite. I had not seen him for years, but I thought why not? Do it for old time's sake."

Johnny Lately had been one of David's first management signings. He had done a good job with Johnny Lately. He changed the teenager's name from Tony Briggs, got him a record deal with the Range label and Johnny Lately had his two minor hits. Then he received a letter from Johnny saying he now wanted new management and David Offen had to move on.

David held no bad memories, especially as a year later the Range label went bankrupt and any royalties and monies owed to Johnny Lately disappeared into the ether, as had his new management.

Johnny Lately needed someone to blame and he cornered David in the street. He heaped abuse at him at the top of his voice, both started grabbing at each other on the pavement, all because of the deal with the Range company.

MCM Plc eventually bought the back catalogue of the Range label, which years later resulted in an unexpected bonus when a big advertisement campaign used an old minor hit by Mr Johnny Lately as a jingle.

Johnny Lately had made an effort for the evening. He wore an expensive-looking sky-blue jacket, his hair had been cut and styled. Johnny Lately was lucky. He had a lot of jet-black hair, brushed back with a thick shiny oil, his hair reflected brightly under the light. He looked very distinctive. He walked straight towards David and Malcolm.

"Thanks for inviting me, David, you're looking well. This is some house, a bit better than that back office in Ellsworth Avenue."

David remembered it well. "Yes, they pulled all that down, new houses now, you're riding high I hear, got a new record out."

"Yes, I wrote it all myself! Again, I hope that I get paid what I am owed this time."

Malcolm didn't smile. "I am sure we have some money in a desk for you. Make sure, now you have had some success, you do not change management. We need to know where to send what is owed."

Johnny stared at the two men as if there was still something to say. "Well, I am going to introduce myself to a few people. Great to see you again, David."

As Johnny walked away, David turned to Malcolm and they each raised their eyebrows. Both knew that Johnny Lately had an album coming out but not much money was going to be spent on it or hope given. If it did not produce sufficient revenue, then that was to be the end of Mr Johnny Lately.

David remembered the downfall of Range Records. It had been an important education. He was surprised how easy it had been to get artists signed to that label; the company itself formed only two years earlier.

Part of the record deal was that their artists would join package tours, promoted by the company.

After several months of touring, everyone was assured they were owed money, but they had to wait. As time passed, people noticed fewer and fewer people were getting paid.

The performers received basic living expenses while on tour. The drivers of the tour bus were getting more.

David searched out Malcolm. The way the wind was blowing, it was becoming obvious what the scam was. Someone got to Johnny early. He dropped off a solicitor's letter stating his management agreement had now ended.

He now had a new deal with Range Management, a subsidiary of Range Records. There was nothing he wanted to say to anyone.

Months later, Range Records filed for bankruptcy. The way the books were written, a few choice people had already been paid everything they were entitled to, which was a lot. The management fees and percentages listed separately as part of the performer's earnings were already drawn from the company accounts and assets.

The artists got little or nothing from what was left, for any records sold or for monies owed from the tours. Some still had outstanding debts. They all were listed as just another set of creditors.

Then came the tax collectors. No one could understand the obligation to pay taxes on money they had never held. It took years to find the paperwork and years before it was eventually sorted out. For some, it had been their only real employment since school.

Malcolm had seen variations on such scams before. "It's a strange thing to witness, it's like buying a fake work of art. The more you invest yourself into it, the more necessary it becomes for you to believe it's all genuine. If you have never had much, you know, money, attention, any idea of a future, then suddenly everything becomes possible, it's easy to just want to ride the wave."

David nodded, "The business can mess you up, that's for sure."

Malcolm looked at the crowd entering the front doors. He saw Derek Ball taking his coat off and waved him over.

"Derek, let me pour you a drink. I have the expensive whiskeys hidden away here behind us."

Derek was chuffed at being singled out. He saw a few faces notice as he casually walked across the room, some turned to see who Malcolm Offen would call by a first name.

Derek nodded to David and Malcolm, "Thank you both for the invitation, I wanted to find a girl to bring tonight. I had an idea the invite might do it for me. Instead, I brought a friend who is desperate to meet you, Brian Nicholls."

Derek turned around. "He just came in with me, but he seems to have disappeared."

Malcolm started pouring a drink. "I met Brian a few months back. He does some studio work for us, correct?"

Malcolm then handed the drink to Derek. "I believe this is what they call the good stuff. I had seen some requests from Brian for an appointment, but I have been very busy. What is it he wants?"

Derek shook his head. "I am not sure, but it appears to be very important, at least to him."

David placed his hand on Derek's shoulder. "I am sure Malcolm will get to him."

"Now in the meantime, there are a lot of very attractive women here tonight. If you get the feeling that any of them is too much car for you to handle, I recommend that you be polite to the waitresses. You might be the only one tonight to do so. Believe me, they will appreciate it."

"Some will also be very impressed that you already have a drink in your hand and are thereby a guest. So, have a little swagger, smile a lot."

Derek beamed at David. "I will bow to your clear expertise in such matters." Derek thanked them both again and left to walk around the garden, perhaps to view some of the flowers there.

# Chapter Six

Janney was 5'4" and slim. Physique-wise, she knew she had a very good posture. The only sport she ever attempted at school was gymnastics. Although she was in good shape, she guessed she would now have to start into an exercise routine, not let herself go.

She thought about her conversation with her mother. It had not come as a surprise. Her mother had taken to repeating herself the last few visits. In truth she would be worried about bringing home any guy to visit her mother. *'If I brought a guy home now, she would more than likely tie him to a chair,'*

*'This house is going to be full of beautiful people*, she thought, *'at least the women will be,'* She recalled a conversation with Malcolm when she first started working for him.

"I don't compete," she remembered saying.

"Then why play?" Malcolm said.

"I like to play," she said, and it rang true for her.

"Then find a game you enjoy," said Malcolm.

*'Yeah,'* she thought, *'let this lot play their own unspoken games. I know who I am; I know what I am, I don't need to win their stupid games'.*

She approached the front gate. She wore a black leather jacket, a small silver stud design on the back, a black top, black jeans, and for an added flourish, she had workman's boots. She had seen a girl walk down a street in Paris, wearing the same outfit. With the way she walked, she never needed to give anyone so much as a sidelong glance.

The security guard at the front gate had been quite taken aback when she presented her invitation. As she entered the house, hands in her pockets, she absorbed all the light around her.

Malcolm spotted Janney as soon as she entered. He nudged David.

"Watch this. Oh! It's going to be hysterical."

Janney waved at Malcolm and then went over to the bar. She stood in front of the woman mixing elaborate drinks and gave her a smile, making it clear 'Whenever you're ready.'

Several women watched Janney enter. They had been engaged in conversation with some very famous faces, or at least had known better to just smile and listen while the other guy talked.

Suddenly a whisper was being made that the black figure at the bar was in fact Janney from the head office.

Several conversations stopped short and with a quick 'excuse me' at a flash, Janney found herself surrounded.

Women around the room looked at the bar and then at each other with a definite 'What the hell just happened?' or 'Who is that?' expression on their faces.

Janney had so many quick requests for her time, with people talking over each other, she had to beg off and say she had important messages to give Malcolm, but she would get right back.

As she left, she could hear everyone talking business behind her. The party suddenly had a new agenda.

Janney approached Malcolm and David with a sly smile. David began to fill a glass.

"Janney, please tell me, you pulled up outside on a motorcycle, a big one, wheels eight feet in front, handlebars above your head. Let me guess, you want a Spanish cocktail, a slice of lemon and lime with a little umbrella."

"One from your famous stash of expensive booze would be nice."

"A woman of taste, I am going to have to invite you more often," said David.

"Indeed," said Malcolm, "I believe you have just become what is known as 'a Face'."

David handed over a drink. "And to all, it entails."

"It's going to mean a lot more work," said Malcolm. "You're going to have to find a way to budget your time."

"And deflect people away from you," said Janney as she raised her glass to Malcolm.

"I had not considered that, but it does rather sound like fun." Malcolm toasted Janney in return.

Janney smiled. This party was going better than she hoped. "How come you two are not surrounded with requests for whatever?"

"They know better. It will soon change after a few drinks, when I start saying hello to people. By the end of the evening, that's when things will really loosen up."

"Sounds like an Irish pub." Janney sipped her drink.

Janney looked at the open back of the house and said, "I am going to check out your garden. Make sure no one chases me."

After Janney walked away, David turned to Malcolm and said with more seriousness than he intended, "You really should find yourself a woman, someone in your own age bracket."

"The best ones are taken." David poured another large whisky. "Anyway, I can be a bad bet."

Janney walked around the lawn area and picked up a plate of food and was surprised at how nice the women she met were. She did not feel out of place.

A few musicians eventually joined Janney in conversation and spoke of the places they played.

Some said that but for all the screaming fans they would have been in trouble with the sound. One laughed and told of a night he had been out of tune the whole concert and found out only when he was packing his guitar away.

The evening was progressing well for everyone. Janney noticed Derek sitting for a while at a bench with a waitress, laughing and joking. It didn't seem to matter to anyone that the girl should have been working.

Unexpectedly, Janney got involved in a long conversation with a young musician.

At first, she thought he was trying his luck. She was about to give him a look to put him straight on the matter, then he started talking about a production of Macbeth he had been to. It had quite an effect on him. "Blew my mind," he said, then he excitedly started explaining the story.

Janney had left school without reading a word of Shakespeare and always kept her mouth shut when the subject was raised. She did not know a single story or any line other than 'to be or not to be,' whatever that meant.

Janney listened and let the young guy talk and talk. She then got caught up with his understanding of the story, the characters. She heard all the motives, the action, the great quotes, how the story changed and finished. She was enjoying herself more and more.

She almost said, '*They should make a film,*' then realised how that sounded. '*I will have to check Shakespeare out,*' she decided. She was beginning to have a great time; it was not just the whisky.

The evening wore on and it might have been that casual friendships were beginning, but Janney thought it would soon be time to make her goodbyes. Suddenly there was a loud scream and she saw people looking towards the top of the house. There was Brian Nicholls standing on a ledge outside the top attic.

Malcolm and David ran into the garden as soon as the scream was heard.

Brian was standing on a still ledge outside the top attic, the bay windows were open, the curtains flew around him in the wind. He seemed to be swaying and staring upwards towards the moon.

Malcolm was about to make a dash for the stairs to get to the attic when suddenly Brian dropped forward without taking a step. Many saw him fall. He broke into an ugly shape.

# Chapter Seven

It took Malcolm and David a few moments to regain their senses. People were running in different directions. Some started making their way to the front door. Derek was on his knees, alone at Brian's side, crying his heart out. His waitress friend had disappeared.

Malcolm and David tore two tablecloths off the tables and covered the body.

Malcolm then ran outside and found two security guards. He brought them up the staircase leading to the attic door.

"The police will be here soon. No one, but absolutely no one, approaches that door, clear?" They both nodded. He clasped their shoulders. "Good men."

David walked around in the middle of the confusion and tried to organise his thoughts. This was going to be a long night. A part of him just wanted to step back and let someone else make decisions.

The moments following Brian's death became stranger and stranger for Janney with each recollection. She wandered around the garden and then into the reception area. She watched people who were shaking and crying. A few were becoming angry for some reason.

She went to comfort Derek, but he was now being led away by someone. With hindsight, she later wondered if she experienced some form of shock. She remembered someone once telling her,

*'If you're in shock, try and recognise yourself as being in shock. It makes things easier to understand.'*

Janney watched the guests. Their behaviour started to appear grotesque. She decided to stay out of everyone's way, see how things played out.

Malcolm came into the garden. His face was a mask.

Malcolm grabbed David's shoulder hard from behind and swung him around.

"Listen! Snap out of it! The police are coming. You must take charge now! These are your people; they will not listen to me. Do not let things get out of control. Make a clear statement; go on record. Protect your interests."

David looked right and left. He nodded and snapped into focus. He called out loudly for any staff within earshot to come to him. He made a quick mental note of those still affected by what happened, they would have to wait. He looked around at those who responded to his call. *'These will do for the moment.'*

"The police are on their way." He looked at the security staff. "Please inform anyone trying to leave that they should remain but do not block their path. Tell the guards down at the gate the same."

"If you see anyone trying to leave, or drive away, don't stop them but tell them that their names will still be given to the police. It would be better for them if they remained to give a statement, get it all finished with."

"Get hold of the paperwork from the door and the front gate. I want the names of everyone invited and the names of everyone that turned up. Get all the car registration numbers."

For all his efforts to show authority, David always felt he would never have the power of command his cousin had. Malcolm seemed to wear it like a jacket.

David took another deep breath. If he was going to take command, he could at least make the pretence. He allowed four or five seconds to reach a decision. David turned and stood square in front of the few catering staff before him.

"I want you all to race around and clean every ashtray. I want anything within an ashtray placed in one of these plastic bags." He picked up some disposable plastic bags.

"Each of you keep a bag. I want any loose cigarette butts you see dropped down picked up and placed in the bags. Look into every bin, empty out any ash you see in any bin."

"Whether or not you have picked up everything, I want you to bring back whatever you have within the bags, back to me, right here! I want you all to return here in three minutes. Then if we have time, we will empty the bags and do it all over again.

"This is a horrible situation. Anyone who wants to sit this out can do so. Do not allow any guest to speak to you harshly. I will remember everyone here who helps me. Now let's all move quickly."

David took a step back. He suddenly realised he had not thought of everything. David walked into the door area bridging the reception and the garden. He raised his voice. This time it had to carry over everyone.

"Everyone, please! The police are on their way. They will be here very soon. They will want to speak to everyone, please wait and do not try to leave." He cleared his throat, "If they determine there is a sufficient reason or a probable cause, they may want to search people."

He saw now he had a lot of undivided attention.

"I would suggest that if you wish to use or lose any prescribed medicines you are holding, then do so now!"

"You may wish to use the bathrooms, or the bins. Please do not throw anything on the floor, or into the bushes."

David looked at the sky. "That may well come back to haunt me," he said quietly.

Malcolm crossed the room and stood beside David. "I suggest you call a lawyer." Both could hear the police and ambulance sirens approaching.

Two waiters approached David and told him they wanted no part of anything further occurring that evening. David just waved them away. "Fine, grab a coffee. You're off the clock."

Janney watched guests and staff pushing to get through the front door. She looked outside, down at the gate and it was clear a bigger crowd was gathering.

Some guests were hurriedly trying to get into their cars, they were prepared to leave behind anyone not ready to go. People were standing around still on the front lawn as if waiting for something to be done on their behalf.

Cars started up, manoeuvring and obstructing each other. The police and an ambulance had quickly arrived, two cars were now blocking the front gate exit. The police told anyone walking down to the gate that no one was leaving.

Three policemen and ambulance staff walked up the footpath. They were met by Malcolm at the door. David was still preoccupied inside with his cleaning detail.

Malcolm smiled and welcomed the police and began giving them essential information, while still blocking the door entrance with his arm. After keeping the police busy for an extra moment or two, he brought them in and walked them over to Brian's covered body.

A few people approached different members of the police, making demands that they had to leave. These were ignored until the senior policeman in charge turned and faced them. He said clearly no one was going to leave.

Malcolm could tell immediately the policeman was ex-army. He had made the statement as fact. Everything said after that was going to be only a conversation.

David walked from the bathroom. As he passed the constables, he dropped an empty plastic bag into a bin.

He walked around whispering to the staff. They could stop working now, wash their hands, go get some coffee, wait till they were called, they were on double time.

What he did not want now was for anyone to be stopped by a policeman, holding a plastic bag full of suspicious roll-ups and asked to explain themselves.

The senior policeman was offered a list with the names of everyone invited that evening. He accepted the list and said a chief inspector was on his way and it was still best to wait—it would not be long.

Janney was still wandering around alone. She saw the police arrive and walked across to Malcolm and David. Neither were now saying much. She looked again outside the window. The front gate was a mass of lights.

A plainclothes inspector approached David and Malcolm. "Good evening, sir. This is your property?"

"Yes, this is my property. I had arranged a party this evening. I have given your man a list of all those invited."

"Some guests brought their own guests. I cannot give you precise details of everyone here, but you should be able to get additional information from those on my list". Mr Evans, the caterer, will have further information for you".

"Thank you, sir, that will be very useful. Can I have your full name please?"

"My name is David Offen."

The inspector wrote the name and all that had been said on his notepad.

"Did you know the deceased?"

"No, sir, I never met the man, nor ever spoke to him."

Malcolm spoke up. "I knew the man, sir. He was invited by a Mr Derek Bell. Mr Bell is still here, I believe, but I am unsure where he is."

"Thank you, sir. Can I please have your full name?"

"My name is Malcolm Offen. I am Mr David Offen's cousin. I am a guest."

Janney stepped forward, "I knew the deceased." At this point, Malcolm put his arm around her shoulders and her tears broke.

The inspector studied Janney for a moment, then said, "Thank you, miss. I may need to speak with you shortly."

Malcolm, David and Janney stood together silently. Janney composed herself. The policemen moved from room to room, appearing surprised at the famous faces they encountered, then into a marked indifference when requesting names, they clearly already knew.

Suddenly Malcolm was jerked out of his thoughts. Confronted with a face, it took an instant to remember.

"Good evening, miss. I am Chief Inspector Hawkins. I will be the senior officer in charge of the investigation into this regrettable incident."

Inspector Hawkins turned towards Malcolm.

"Hello, Major. It's been a while."

# Chapter Eight

Janney stood between the three men. She suddenly felt aware of her size. The three men were each over six feet tall. This by itself would not have been strange but she felt a different energy. She felt aware it was very male. Whatever it was, it seemed very powerful.

Inspector Hawkins stood calm and straight and watched both Malcolm and David with what some would call an inscrutable smile. David was glaring at the inspector with clear focused hostility. Malcolm looked completely shaken.

The four were silent for four or five seconds and then Malcolm composed himself. "Hawkins! Excuse me! Bill! Good grief! Quite a surprise. You're in the police?"

The inspector's smile broadened. "Chief inspector!"

"Good grief, well, where are my manners? Bill, this is Janney Malone, my work colleague, where I work. This is my cousin, David Offen. This is his house." Janney stared at Malcolm. This was the first time she had ever heard him stammer.

"Your cousin, really! Mr Offen and I have met before, at this house in fact."

"He had not been invited." David stared at Malcolm as if expecting a statement.

Malcolm regained a little more composure.

"Janney, this is Bill Hawkins. We were in the Army together."

Inspector Hawkins smiled and nodded to Janney. He watched David and seemed to enjoy his discomfort. He turned back to Malcolm.

"We ate some of the same dirt, right, Major? We last saw each other when I boarded that ship in '45. I heard you went to America."

"That's right, back a few years now."

Janney smiled at each of them, *'All fine gentlemen together,'* she thought to herself. *I wonder when Brian is going to intrude into this little reunion.'*

Inspector Hawkins looked around the room and then said, "Well, Major! I have several things I must check on, but I will return very shortly. I will need to speak with all of you."

"Well, take your time," said David, "we are not going anywhere."

Inspector Hawkins spoke to three policemen standing at the front door. He then called over each policeman who had been speaking with guests.

Once the constables were pulled aside, each policeman opened out their notepad and began reporting to the inspector. David continued to glare towards the inspector with the same hostility as before. He turned quietly to Malcolm but still could hardly pull his attention away.

"How well do you know him?"

Malcolm studied David, "Calm yourself down. I knew him well once; I hadn't seen him for 21 years. How on earth do you know him?"

"He appeared backstage at a concert event a few months ago, just burst in and said he had a warrant to search for drugs. He found some, as it happened there was quite a lot. Two of the band were found in possession, neither could continue the tour. Visas revoked. Cost them a lot of work. He even applied to have the venue's licence removed."

David looked intently at Malcolm. Malcolm stared back. David felt embarrassed. He began to calm down.

"Two weeks later, he turned up at this house, my house! during a dinner party. He said he had a warrant and questions. I could choose to answer them there or at the station. I had to call a lawyer, right there on the spot! while I had dinner guests waiting."

David began coming down from his anger at the appearance of Inspector Hawkins. Suddenly both cousins noticed Janney. She watched their faces and then saw a whole different style of manners kick in.

David blurted out, "Janney, I apologise, cleaning linen in public and all that. This is all unimportant stuff, really, I should have spoken more appropriately. Right now, is not the time for such talk."

Janney felt a compulsion to just keep staring at David Offen.

'*Get over yourself,*' was all she thought. She looked again at his polite face. '*There is a poor guy dead in the garden and this idiot is interested in his manners, some sort of pathetic upper-class role-play he carries around for himself.*' A role-play she deeply felt she would never be interested in learning about, or even hearing about.

Janney started getting angrier at each time she heard conversations around her reverting back to the interests of whoever was speaking.

Perhaps it was the shock she felt earlier, maybe others were feeling the same, maybe not. She suddenly stopped to check herself. '*Why on earth am I being bothered to give these people any sort of credit?*'

Malcolm realised he left two security guards at the attic staircase and raced across the room. He ran upstairs and found they were gone and replaced by a policeman. The two spoke. No one had entered the attic since the death.

David watched Inspector Hawkins talking with his officers and saw his face change. Brian's body was being lifted by stretcher into the ambulance.

Inspector Hawkins ran up the back of the ambulance and spoke to the attendants inside. Two ambulance staff left the back of the ambulance with him, the doors slammed shut. The ambulance slowly began moving back down towards the front gate.

Inspector Hawkins brought two constables inside. He instructed them to stand by the buffet tables. "No one is to touch anything on these tables, the abandoned drinks, empty cups, glasses, food, nothing!" He then walked straight towards David and Malcolm.

"I need a separate room where people can speak with medical staff privately, then you can bring me to the room Mr Nicholls jumped from." Inspector Hawkins was no longer making requests.

David said the television room was available. The inspector curtly asked where he could find the television room, then went back to the ambulance staff left waiting at the door and brought them back inside the house.

He called over two constables and introduced the ambulance crew. He pointed at the television room and gave instructions.

He returned to David and spoke in a marked brusque manner, "Right. Now I would appreciate being shown the room where the fall took place."

David and the inspector walked up the staircase. They approached the attic steps.

Malcolm was still there, still speaking with the policeman at the door. He stood aside.

"Bill, is there anything else we can do to help?"

"Very well, Major. Both of you follow everything I say. Do not touch any part of the door to this attic or any part of these steps, or anything else I point at for that matter. Stay here till I return" He stared at David Offen. "Those are very serious instructions, Mr Offen."

# Chapter Nine

The inspector moved the guard at the steps aside and spoke privately. He then climbed three steps to the attic door. He pushed down the end of the long metal door handle with a pencil, pushed the attic door open with the same pencil and entered the room.

The room was still lit by a single bulb. The inspector could see boxes had been stored there for some time. There was thick undisturbed dust on some boxes, an inch thick. The bay windows were wide open, pulled inwards. The windows were more than seven feet high.

The inspector studied the metal handles on the windows and the window frame without touching them. Curtains still blew inside and out. There was no balcony beyond the window, just a small sill with a sheer drop, where Brian last stood.

The inspector saw a telescope and tripod in one of the boxes, still sealed, dust covered the packing, never used. '*Probably just an idea he had,*' thought the inspector.

There was a very heavy wooden chair, with armrests facing the open windows.

The inspector looked hard at the floor and the dust on the floor around the legs of the chair.

He could see by the dust around one of the legs, the chair had been very recently moved, part of an inch or so. He noted there were different shoeprints in the dust as well as his own. He examined the different shoe marks.

Inspector Hawkins realised he could easily contaminate evidence. He carefully left the room, again taking minimal use of the door handle. Inspector Hawkins descended the short attic stairs. He saw David and Malcolm waiting expectantly.

The inspector started brushing dust from his coat onto the floor. It was difficult to lose all the dust. "Well, sir, I am afraid I am going to have to bring a rather extensive forensic team here to examine this room as well as elsewhere within the house."

David stared blankly. With complete puzzlement, he calmly spoke. "Could you please tell me what is going on? The poor fellow jumped to his death. We all saw it. Is there still something to know?"

Inspector Hawkins looked at both David and Malcolm. His face showed quiet contempt as he turned to David.

"I still have several questions to ask. I have yet to decide whether to place anyone under caution. I need to speak to all your guests. I trust you will have no objection to that. I will be returning to you shortly; you can hold your questions until then."

The inspector pointed at the staircase and then told Malcolm and David to walk ahead downstairs. The inspector waited back a few moments then followed. Malcolm spoke quietly as they descended the staircase, "Did you call your lawyer?"

David stared down, then said, "Yes, good suggestion. Oh! I better check the gate. Maybe he can't get in."

David walked through the house to the front door and noticed things had calmed down a little. People were sitting on a few deck chairs put out on the grass and talking. He walked down to the front gate and saw his lawyer, Mike Fallon, leaning against his car, waiting. Once David spoke to the constables at the gate, he got Mike Fallon ushered in.

Mike Fallon was a young-looking 28-year-old lawyer whom David had used in a few situations during the last few years. He was a lawyer David knew would come immediately, whenever called upon, day or night.

David trusted Mike, most of the time he enjoyed his company, he had complete confidence in him as a lawyer. On several occasions, David found Mike so annoying he had considered strangling him. Mike's primary specialism was criminal law. David had called Mike for advice and help during his two previous meetings with Inspector Hawkins.

David returned with Mike, approached Malcolm and Janney and introduced them. David started to bring Mike up to date. Mike stopped David, then said, "Listen, there is more going on here than we are being told."

Mike stopped David again from interrupting. "Are you aware another ambulance has been called? I heard it confirmed while waiting outside."

David caught his breath. He spoke aloud for anyone to hear. "What! Right! I want some answers. I want to know what is going on and I want to know now!" It was clear to everyone in the room David was raising his voice for no apparent purpose. He started to walk around Mike. "This is my house and I accept the police have a job to do but this is still my house."

David was about to race to find Inspector Hawkins. Malcolm moved quickly and blocked his path and again told him to calm down. Malcolm was ready to bring down some authority upon David. He was becoming obnoxious.

Mike then moved beside David. "Listen, we are limited in our options. They are in charge, they outnumber us. They are not impressed by shouting and anger; they are familiar with it. They get bored with it."

David stood back; he spent a few seconds composing himself. "What do you suggest?"

Mike relaxed, "Let me do the talking. I may have to do some quick fishing around." Mike nodded to Malcolm and Janney and walked away.

Janney watched David try to relax a little, then tried to offer a little encouragement. "Well, he seems to know what he is about."

David turned sharply on Janney. His voice was still a little hyped up. "Just never get into long conversations with him. When he feels like it, he can turn into the biggest freak I have ever met."

Janney watched Mike; she watched him walk the room. He went straight into groups of people, standing, smiling then talking. No one appeared surprised or put off by the intrusion. At this moment, he appeared a lot more at ease than either David or Malcolm.

After about 15 minutes of walking around, David, Malcolm and Janney saw Mike suddenly break from the group and walk quickly towards Inspector Hawkins. The inspector had entered alone, examining his notes.

Janney had never seen anyone behave like Mike. She could not decide if the easy confidence he had standing in front of the inspector was real, or if it was some sort of performance.

It was clear Inspector Hawkins was still angry. His face showed aggression. Mike, on the other hand, continued to just stand there, still calm, seemingly unaware of the behaviour. Once they finished, Mike casually walked back to David.

"You're in a lot of trouble, David. Your guests will be allowed to leave shortly. Except for those that will be taken to hospital. There are three in your TV room, being treated right now."

David stepped back. He appeared speechless. Malcolm then asked, "What else can you tell us?"

"There will be a forensic team arriving soon, a large one. The inspector will be questioning you all at the station, I will try and sort something out. This house will be full of police for the next several hours."

Janney could not see the logic of it all. "Why me? Poor Brian jumped. I never saw him all night."

Mark addressed them all. "You three and possibly others are only witnesses' now, realise this when speaking with that man—he will not be denied. Here he comes again."

Inspector Hawkins walked into the group.

"I am sure Mr Fallon has told you that I require all of you to attend the station."

Before either David or Malcolm could open their mouths, Mike stopped them short.

"Inspector, we are in the early hours now. Mr Offen has to say goodbye to his guests. If we leave for the station now, it will hours before you get a report from your forensic experts and the medical team, hours before you are able to begin questioning anyone. You will be tired, we will be tired, anything said will be affected by that. Any statements, recollections or interview notes will be later examined with that in mind, maybe even challenged or changed."

Mike allowed for a moment of consideration.

"Everyone is cooperating, everyone will continue to cooperate. Can we make an appointment to see you later today? My client can book into a hotel now and meet you at the station. Choose a time. More information will then be available, more informed questions, everyone will be refreshed, tempers cooled?"

Inspector Hawkins was thinking hard. He was concentrating more on this lawyer than David or Malcolm. It was clear he was debating something within himself.

"Very well." He turned to David. "Please attend to me at the station at 3 pm today." The inspector pulled out a card and handed it to Mike. "Here is the station's address." He turned to Malcolm.

"Sorry to drag you into this, Major. I have your contact address and yours, Miss Malone. I will be in touch with both of you to arrange an interview."

"Quite all right, Bill. For goodness' sake, it should be Malcolm by this time."

"Very well, Malcolm. I am glad we have met again. Mr Offen, once we have finished here, your house will be left secure. I will give you more details at the station." The inspector abruptly turned and walked away.

David was fit to burst to say something. Mike turned again and raised palms in front of him.

"David, say nothing. That man is not your fan. He is not going to be a friend. We just received a concession; do not let it slip away by getting into his face."

"Listen to the man," said Malcolm. "Let's get out of here."

David finally agreed and got his coat. He numbly walked to the front door. He saw three guests leaving, three women.

They were leaving the TV room and walking towards the ambulance.

He suddenly realised who they were. Two of them were the teenage daughters of an influential theatre impresario, he had called the man personally and given an assurance he would safely take care of his daughters if they attended tonight. The third girl was their visiting cousin from America.

The three girls were being guided towards the ambulance, their arms were held by others as they walked, they appeared slightly uncoordinated, they were trying to speak but did not seem to be speaking to those guiding them, they were helped up the stairs of the ambulance.

Once the ambulance pulled away, everyone stood in the driveway. It was cold but the air seemed clean. It woke them awake a little. David and Mike arranged where and when to meet later that day. David got into Malcolm's car without another word.

Janney realised she had no transport. Mike immediately spotted the situation and offered a lift. Janney thanked him and followed Mike down to the gate to find his car.

# Chapter Ten

Malcolm drove into the traffic. He saw David staring into the distance.

"You stay with me tonight."

David nodded, "Just how well do you know Hawkins?"

"He was a sergeant under me during the war. Stopped me going to pieces a couple of times."

"I can't imagine you ever going to pieces."

"There are no tough guys, Dave."

David sat in the car, watching the night lights. He tried to process all that happened. "This could mean a lot of trouble for me."

Malcolm was silent for a moment. "For both of us, just how good is this Fallon guy?"

"He is good. I trust him. He is aware of his limits. He can see where and when heavyweights are needed and can call them in, if necessary, always puts the client first."

"Good if you can find people like that. Something else happened tonight besides the death. You and I need to talk about the three girls; also, those two other incidents, the raid at the venue and the warrant at your dinner party."

"Why? You think any of its relevant?

"You have had a lot of bad luck lately, David, maybe someone doesn't like you. Maybe someone stole all your good luck totems, you might need to buy some more."

"Hawkins has never liked me, but he was angry tonight."

"I saw Bill get angry a few times. Most of the time he never had to. He was always the man in charge. The times I saw him very angry was when he saw civilians suffering, being vulnerable or helpless. Or if people started making boring excuses for situations, or their behaviour. He can become very angry, when people shrug their shoulders, as if some things don't matter. He has a big heart."

"Yeah, well, I have a big heart as well, but it never won me a card game. What am I talking about? I have done nothing wrong. I don't like dealing with the police, especially Hawkins. He acts like there is no one in charge except him, as if he has the big advantage."

Malcolm began to park the car. "Listen, Dave, firstly, the police are always in charge, they always have the big advantage. They carry it two feet in front of them. Bill is a very fair man. At least that is what I remember. Do not argue or debate with him. Give him everything, everything! Believe me, if you try to negotiate or hold stuff back, he will jump on you with hobnail boots and the conversation will start all over again. Leave the important stuff to that lawyer of yours. If he really is a friend, he will have your interests. Also, tell him Bill is a very clever man. When he starts to look into your eyes, believe me, he knows all about you."

Malcolm and David entered Malcolm's townhouse. Both had a series of drinks and talked. David became very drunk and went to the bedroom. He got on top of the bed and slept still dressed. It was 5 am.

Janney discovered Mike lived across the river near her. She only wanted to get to the night buses, but Mike said he would drive her the whole way.

Mike turned to Janney and said, "Are you tired?"

Janney realised she was wide awake. She knew sleep was not going to be easy.

"No, why?"

"There is an all-night cafe across the bridge. The early hours market workers use it. We could get a coffee. Might be a good idea to talk."

Janney said that was ok. She could go for a coffee.

Mike parked the car. There was still winter darkness. They walked past several covered stalls and entered the café. It was mostly empty. Mike went to the counter and Janney noticed the elderly woman behind the counter quickly lost her frown and smiled at Mike. They seemed to know each other.

Mike turned to Janney. "How do you like it?"

Janney told him and he brought two cups to the table.

Mike stirred his cup. "So how well did you know Brian Nicholls?"

"Not well."

"Did he come with anyone tonight?"

"That's how he got a ticket. He came with Derek Ball as his plus one."

"Oh, like that?"

"No, Brian asked him as a favour."

"So, if he just wanted to mix with celebrities, why did he disappear upstairs?"

"I don't know."

"Miss Malone, excuse me if it looks like I am questioning you. I have no right to do that. This is just an effort to gather information. Please stop me if I appear rude."

"That's ok. It really does not make sense. Derek told me Brian only wanted to attend the party so he could get to talk to Malcolm, but he never tried to."

Mike went silent. He stared into his coffee.

"What is Brian's background? What did he do?"

"He works occasionally for the company, within the recording studios."

"Sort of on a casual locum basis?"

"Yes, he is a musician and musical arranger. He helps where he can. He is often asking for work. I have heard that he is very good. People seem to like him. Most of the time he is a bartender at the Back Door."

"I have seen that place. It's near here."

Mike thought again for a moment, watching the table. He then appeared to reach a decision.

"Miss Malone, may I call you Janney?"

"Of course."

"I want to get back to my flat and rest up for the trip to the station. Would it be possible for you and me to visit the Back Door, Monday evening, Can I call you?"

"You want to visit the Back Door with me?"

"Yes, do you know anyone there who knew Brian?"

"I know the manager."

"Can you introduce me?"

Janney felt she was getting more involved in the whole business than she had expected. She had left David's house just wanting to get home to bed.

She saw the option now was to distance herself. She was about to say it all had nothing to do with her. That thought rang bells in her head as a bad idea.

"Yeah, ok! I could introduce you to the guy."

"Let's arrange to meet. If you like, we can get something to eat first." Janney looked at this new guy she had just met and without really thinking she thought, '*Why not?*'

She also felt something was going on. She had a feeling she had just been pulled around and persuaded into doing something.

"Yeah, sure," she said. She looked hard at this guy and in a flash found herself thinking, '*What's with this lack of guile act? Who does he think he's impressing?*'

She wondered if this was just his technique. She was watching him carefully and from somewhere she heard her mother say, '*Thieves think everyone steals.*' She heard her mother say it might apply to her.

Janney had no answer to that. She needed time to understand what it all meant or how it was supposed to even apply to her. She always trusted her mother. She knew now, lately she started resisting her.

Slowly she began to think a little clearer. She knew she had been putting up walls for a long time. It had kept her feeling safe. '*I wonder what that says about me. Maybe I just want to feel comfortable. When did feeling comfortable become important?*' Her mother's voice was really starting to haunt her.

She needed to get away and think. The shock of the last few hours was allowing her a few new thoughts to play with. Mike sat with a calmness Janney rarely saw.

'*Maybe this guy is a phoney,*' she thought, '*But maybe I can give him a little rope. Maybe he's only a phoney on weekends.*'

The conversation turned to the events of the evening. Neither asked for more information about the other. The cafe started to fill up. It was time to leave.

Mike drove Janney to her door. He asked for her work number.

He said he would call on Monday; they could arrange to meet up then. Janney left the car and stood on the pavement, watching him drive away. Something inside made her feel, somehow, she had turned a corner.

# Chapter Eleven

David and Mike had agreed to meet in a pub across the road from the police station. Mike knew the landlord. They allowed themselves an hour before the interview.

"Any more thoughts on last night?" Mike asked as he brought drinks to the table.

"The papers have it already. It will be across the Monday morning editions. I had a newspaper call and they asked for a comment on a story it all happened because everyone was stoned out of their minds."

Mike gave a face as if to say, '*So what*?' He then leaned forward. "Hawkins is going to try and trip you up, get you to keep talking and possibly incriminate yourself. I must do the important talking. If I raise my hand, like this. wrist on the table, fingers upward, you turn silent, immediately ok!"

"OK! OK! Look, I do not know where they are going with this drug angle, but I cannot be charged with anything relating to a drug offence."

"If I am refused an entry visa to another country, especially America, or if any of the venues I deal with start refusing to deal with me, or if the bands, their managers, anyone, start to avoid me as being nothing but trouble, the whole house of cards could collapse."

"How so?"

"Anyone can promote a show or a tour, its necessary to control the venues. You need leverage where you promise a continuing flow of business. or threaten otherwise. I deal with promoters around the world who all operate as I do; we scratch each other's backs. If they smell blood in the water, I will be squeezed out, it could happen very quickly."

"The major acts are international—they have no loyalty. As for the rest, whichever promoter offers the best act, the best deal, the most money, especially the most grease, they get the contract. Once I become bad news, a bad association, more trouble than I am worth, any connections I have abroad become worthless. No one will take my calls."

"David, you have to try not to hold on to the past and to want to manipulate the future."

"I knew it! I knew it. You're going to drift into that Zen malarkey again. Listen! You just focus on what you're being paid for."

"Life is constantly changing. Open yourself up to the natural flow of life. Try and follow the arrows that also fly past the tree; don't only study the target."

David was ready to jump out of his chair. "What on this green earth does that even mean? You drive me mad with this stuff. Listen! Now! This is me talking now, stop it, please, I am in real trouble here."

"Alright Dave, look at me. Look into my eyes. Calm down, I want your mind to go blank. You saw nothing, you know nothing."

"Too right, I know nothing. I am in the wilderness here."

Mike spoke softly to David. "Hawkins is going to demand answers, answers you will carefully consider."

"Hear me! Take your time to consider all the questions; that's your right. He will pressure you; he will ask you, "Why do you need time to consider?" "Why do you hesitate?" You have the answers, and he wants answers now! Tell him you are taking time to consider so you can be accurate. Do not get hurried, do not get thrown by anything said, even if what you are told, you happen to know to be grossly untrue. Remember that is often only a tactic and will be done deliberately."

"It's an old trick to get you to keep talking, to keep your answering, to keep responding. Remember, this is not an argument, not a debate, not a negotiation. Some people carry a stupid arrogance. They believe that if it's necessary to agree on the facts of a situation then the truth or the facts become a gift to bargain with. That there are no facts, just interpretations."

Mike could see David's mind was wandering. "Hear me when I say this, when you sit in a police station, all that becomes rubbish. This is his game, his home ground, he knows how the game is played. He has been here many times before. All we have on our side is that we will play at our own speed. Don't worry, in a little while it will be over."

Mike sat back in his chair. "Let's just cool down, feel the circulation in your arms. It's a nice pub! Live in the moment. All the moments you have are valuable."

David started taking easier breaths. "Thanks Mike, but I do not care about the pub. Please do not go off on one of your Zen trips now. I need you to focus on my interests."

"I am not asking you to embrace the nothingness within life. No need to look towards the infinite."

Mike slowly smiled, "Try not to look back in anger, try instead to look around the edges with awareness. It's all a lie hidden within a joke."

"Look, that is the sort of talk that scares me. I really need to feel you are on planet Earth when we go into the station."

Mike laughed. "It's all ok, Dave, I was just getting in touch with my inner lawyer. Believe me, it's going to be alright. As you say, you have done nothing wrong. At least nothing that will ever trouble your conscience much."

David knew Mike had never let him down, so he resisted an urge to throw his drink in his face.

He realised then that his anxiety had peaked and had dropped away minutes ago. He had little worry left about the interview. David wondered if this had been what Mike had always intended. He could really hate Mike if he started to believe he was that clever.

They finished their drinks and then got up to leave. David looked around and thought '*Mike is right, it is a nice pub*'. They crossed an empty road for the interview.

They entered the station. The reception area was empty, except for the duty officer behind the front desk.

David approached the front desk and said respectfully, "Good day, we have an appointment to see Inspector Hawkins at 3 o'clock. My name is David Offen."

As the desk officer retreated to the back office to pass the message, Mike said softly, "Not sure if *'an appointment'* were the correct words to use. If they keep us waiting for an hour or two, it will not trouble them much." Mike looked around, he did not know this station, but he knew it better than David Offen ever would.

They sat on the two wooden chairs in the reception area, and then at 3pm on the dot, at least according to the large wall clock, Inspector Hawkins appeared and invited them both into an interview room. They sat down across from each other, a heavy wooden table between them, a single bare light bulb hanging overhead.

The inspector placed a folder and notebook to his right and left.

"Thank you for coming, Mr Offen."

"Glad to be of assistance."

"I have a number of questions about all that occurred yesterday evening at your house."

"From the information we have gathered, between 60 and 70 people attended the party at your house, together with extra security and caterers. Would that be accurate?"

David allowed himself time to answer. He took an obvious breath, "Sounds accurate. You might have better information than I have. Everyone who attended had an invitation. Some brought their own guest, some might have brought two, I am unsure. I did not take the names of the extra guests."

"Did you know Mr Nicholls?"

"I had never met the man. He was a guest of a guest."

"Who would have access to the attic?"

"I imagine anyone. Many of the rooms on the upper floors were locked. I did not want guests wandering into any room they liked. It was my home after all. The attic was always unlocked."

"The attic had a great deal of dust. How often was it cleaned?"

"Hardly ever, I suppose. It was used for storage, boxes and such. I used to go up there sometimes, stare out of the windows and read, but not since the summer. As you say, it was very dusty."

"We often played loud music downstairs, like we had at the party. The vibrations create more dust."

"Do you normally leave the attic windows open?"

"Never, pigeons would fly in, leave a mess."

"So, they are normally closed?"

"Yes, there is a latch you pull down, you would have seen it, kept the windows closed tight. Prevents the wind from making them rattle."

"Thank you, Mr Offen, this is all very helpful."

"Now! Mr Offen, we treat every suicide as a suspicious death. There are still some important questions I must ask in respect of the events following Mr Nicholls' death."

"Go ahead."

"Once Mr Nicholls fell from the attic, I believe you ordered all ashtrays and bins emptied and cleaned."

Mike raised his fingers from the table and David sat back.

"Inspector, with due respect, how can Mr Nicholls' fall be related to the ashtrays?"

"I will get to that. I wanted to ask if Mr Offen would offer an explanation. It seems a strange thing to concentrate upon, following such a tragic event."

David relaxed in his chair. "Well, it was all such a shock, I might have even been in shock. I was breathing hard and smelt all the used ash from the ashtrays around me. It disgusted me, I just ordered them clean. What difference does it make?"

"During the course of our investigations, four used marijuana cigarettes were found."

David waved a hand, "Really! 70 odd guests, young guests, pop stars, celebrities and someone brought some marijuana. Hardly surprising. Only four turned up, you say."

Inspector Hawkins examined his folder. "Remember there had been a clean-up, from all the ashtrays and the bins. The ash from any cigarettes were not found. It was disposed of somewhere, with who knows what else, it has even been suggested, down into your own toilets."

David relaxed. He was enjoying the inspector's frustration. "So, you say."

Mike raised his fingers again, "Inspector, you did not ask us here on a Sunday to discuss ashtrays?"

"No! I am now conducting a murder investigation. Mr Nicholls died with a substantial amount of active LSD in his system, the equivalent of 25 to 40 tablets of LSD. I have reason to believe Mr Nicholls had not been alone in the attic."

David and Mike were both silent. Mike was the first to speak. "I feel you have more to say, Inspector."

"Indeed, upon examination of the punch bowl on your buffet table, the punch itself also contained a large quantity of LSD, again between 25 and 30 tablets. Several half-empty glasses left on tables in the garden also held quantities of LSD."

The inspector paused; he was watching for a reaction. "Three of your guests drank from the punch bowl. They were not aware of its full contents, so each became affected by the drug, clearly a very bad experience. You saw them all taken to hospital."

Inspector Hawkins began speaking with greater emphasis.

"You can certainly now appreciate my questions and that your actions at the party following the death of Mr Nicholls may be viewed as very pertinent to the investigation."

David had stopped breathing. He then began taking deep breaths. Mike was still looking at the inspector. He turned to speak to David. The sight stopped him immediately.

Mike spoke with a new insistence across the table. "Inspector! In the light of what you have just told my client, I would ask for an opportunity to speak with my client alone. Right Now! some water might be useful."

The inspector looked intently at them both, then stood up and collected his papers. As he walked around the desk, he told them to call the constable outside when they were ready to resume. He left the room without another word.

# Chapter Twelve

David was staring at his hands. "How could this happen?" He started to blubber, his face creased, the tears began to pour uncontrollably. He raised his hands to his face. Mike had seen this before, nearly always in police stations. David was not going to answer questions for a little while.

Mike spoke gently, "Dave! I am going to get you some water. Take regular breaths and breathe deeply. Try and concentrate on a spot on the wall. Listen to me, I am being serious, stop thinking about what has been said. Stare at a spot on the wall. Try relaxing your arms. I will only be a minute."

Mike knocked on the door, he told the officer he was getting some water. He walked into the back room behind the front desk. He told those sitting there he needed to use a telephone. Inspector Hawkins was by the door and nodded approval to the desk officer.

Mike called Malcolm Offen and said his cousin needed a friendly face at the police station. He said David might be having an emotional breakdown. Malcolm said he would be there as soon as he could.

Mike asked for some water for David. Again, Inspector Hawkins nodded to an officer with approval.

Mike walked across the room to the inspector and others standing there. He spoke in a voice meant to be carried.

"You're getting nothing further from my client for the time being. He is unable to answer your questions until he composes himself. I doubt that will be today. Unless you have charges to bring, we will have to postpone this witness interview. I may call a doctor if I believe it necessary." He turned away with no interest at any reply.

Mike saw a small kitchen sink where the staff made tea. He picked up a cup and began filling it. He turned and spoke again. "I have arranged for transport. Once it arrives, we will be leaving, unless as I said, you wish to change the parameters of the interview." He walked away again without waiting for an answer.

Mike returned to David; he gave him the water to drink. David held the cup in both hands.

"Dave, mate, I am trying to get you out of here, Malcolm is on his way. I am hoping having Malcolm here is just enough to get you out."

David gave a weak smile. He was no longer blubbering, but the tears still fell down his face.

Mike looked at David without speaking. He tried to help David stand, he said, "OK! Time for you to find yourself again. David! let me take you into the bathroom. You need to wash your face. Look in a mirror. Come on, stand up."

Davis stood upright. He turned to Mike, he said, "Sorry," he gave a shy look.

Mike pulled the chair back. "That's fine, tears have a purpose; that purpose has passed. Let's get you straight before Malcolm sees you."

Mike brought David out of the interview room and into the bathroom.

"Give your face a good wash, use cold water, rinse your mouth out. Doing normal things will make the world seem normal, make you feel normal again. Go on, splash your face again. Scrub your fingernails; they are dirty. Use the brush."

David hunched himself over. He did all that Mike said. He was not thinking, Mike was giving orders, he was taking orders.

He started to examine his fingernails, they were dirty, and they needed a scrubbing. '*I should do that*'. The world started to emerge again.

After a few moments, David stood upright, fixed his coat collar and looked in the mirror. He was standing in a bathroom. He was David Offen, a big-time music promoter. He turned to Mike, "Thanks, man. Thanks a lot. Give me a minute."

There was silence for a moment or two, then he turned and opened the door, held it open for Mike. They both walked into the corridor and were silent. They looked for the inspector.

David saw the inspector. He was talking to three constables. He thought, '*No point in privacy anymore,*' He approached the inspector, stayed a distance so as not to intrude into their conversation, he waited until the inspector was ready.

Inspector Hawkins turned and approached David and Mike without a word.

"Inspector, what you said, it came as a great surprise, a big shock! Lost my way for a few moments. Thank you for your patience."

"Quite alright."

"I am still a little thrown by this, quite a lot actually." David moved his feet and attempted to stand a little taller.

"I want you to be aware, Inspector, I will answer all questions, I will cooperate in every way possible, without reservation. I will make all possible enquiries and will bring you any information, rumour, gossip, lie told, refusal to talk or anything at all I discover. I will bring everything!"

"That's good to hear."

"Someone invaded my home. They assaulted people within my home, young innocents! People I had invited to sit at my table, eat my food. A man died in my house, someone killed a man in my house; while I was there, I watched it happen. I want this person found, Inspector. They cannot walk the streets, whoever they are."

Inspector Hawkins just nodded his head.

"I must ask something of you, Inspector, I need you to grant me a small respite, allow me a day or two to pull my thoughts together. I will return whenever you wish, as many times as you wish. You can knock on my door whenever you wish."

"Very well, Mr Offen, I will contact you again in a day or so. Thank you for coming in. Mr Fallon will be taking you home?"

"Yes, I have transport. Before I go, have you any information on my guests, those taken to hospital? How are they?"

"As far as I am aware, they have recovered, to an extent anyway. They spent several hours at the hospital. Their families took them home around midday today.

"Thank you."

Mike spoke over David's shoulder, "Most gracious. Thank you. We have transport coming. We will wait in your reception area."

Everyone exchanged some sort of look towards each other. Dignity somehow rose from wherever it still existed.

David and Mike went to the reception area and sat on the chairs they had first waited upon. After another 10 minutes, Malcolm walked through the door.

"Hello, David, how is the boy?"

"Thanks for coming, Malcolm. Lots to say. Let's get out of here, Mike! You can follow in your car."

Malcolm looked at the reception desk and saw Inspector Hawkins through the door leading to the back office. He asked the desk officer if he could speak with the inspector. The inspector saw Malcolm and came out.

"Hello Bill, I would have preferred to catch up over drinks, but when would be best for you for me to come in, give you what little I know?"

Inspector Hawkins smiled. This was a conversation he had wanted. "Is tomorrow ok for you, give it to last a couple of hours, about 1pm? No need for a lawyer. You will need to have a long talk with your cousin. He has a lot to tell you."

"Good, 1pm is good for me. A couple of hours, you say?" They shook hands. "Great that you're ok, Bill."

The three men left the station, got in the two cars and then drove to Malcolm's house. David told Malcolm everything that had been said. Malcolm had questions that no one could answer. Mike just listened; the questions had been useful. He was glad Malcolm was on board. No one would try anything with him around.

# Chapter Thirteen

Janney rose earlier than usual on Monday morning. She had decided she would get a coffee in a coffee bar, read all the newspapers, get up to speed, if that was even possible, get her head ready before getting to work.

The newspapers all had one story on their front pages. No surprise there, reasoned Janney, they did have all of Sunday to get it ready.

There were lots of suggestive comments about what had happened at the party, drug-filled debauchery as well as relationship fights. There were black and white photographs of the guests desperately leaving in a hurry, some on foot, pushing through the front gates. It was clear the newspapers had only basic details. There was little background information on poor Brian Nicholls.

What they did seem to have, much to Janney's surprise, was a lot of information about David Offen. She had never seen an article written specifically about David before, but now she saw full-page reports in three different papers with statements that carried an inference that he was somehow infamous or dangerous.

As Janney entered the office building that morning, she felt every eye as she walked the staircase and corridor.

She approached her desk, but Malcolm quickly appeared from his room and pointed inside, he walked back inside, leaving the door open. This time she was sure of it—everybody was looking at her.

Malcolm went by the kettle, making them both coffees. He looked over his shoulder, "How do you feel?"

"Bit better."

Malcolm brought Janney a coffee and sat behind his desk.

"Have you read the papers?"

"Yeah, a few."

"It's clear they do not have the facts. That will no doubt change. I want your assurance that you will not be giving any interviews. Has anyone contacted you?"

"No, I don't give interviews. I don't know anything anyway."

"Do not even tell anyone that! Do not discuss in any way anything you saw happen or what you think happened. Discuss it with no one. If you do, the papers will chase your friends or family for a quote."

Janney thought of her mother. Her mother had not called. She thought of the new answer phones that were now on the market. *'Maybe I should get one.'*

Janney pulled herself out of her rambling thoughts. She still had to focus. She had questions she could ask, but nothing essential.

Malcolm was watching Janney concentrate. She was looking up and down from her lap. "Listen, relax!" he said sharply. Malcolm was drawing her full attention.

"We have additional information. This is private information; I do not expect it to be private for long."

"I am going to tell you something because you should know it all, but also so that when you're confronted with it you will not be surprised."

Janney tried to relax. She gave a passing thought to how strange it is to have to try to relax, only because someone suggested it, or in Malcolm's case ordered it. She could see Malcolm was priming himself for one of his bullet point conversations.

"The police are treating Brian's death as a murder investigation. He was made to swallow a large quantity of LSD. He died while under the influence of LSD, probably why he fell. Someone had been in that attic with him. A large amount of LSD had been placed in the punch bowl at the party. Three people drank from the bowl. They were the ones taken to hospital. Maybe the same person who gave Brian the LSD also put tablets in the punch bowl. Now take a few minutes."

Janney did not seem to feel anything at what she heard. She felt as if she was just taking orders. *'Poor Brian,'* crossed her thoughts.

"Poor Brian," she said quietly.

"Exactly," said Malcolm. "Let's never forget that he is the victim here and somewhere out there is a predator."

Malcolm gave Janney some space. "You saw all that was written about David. It's clear the story is being somehow managed. It becomes more important now that you're never misquoted, or even quoted at all."

Malcolm had his whole attention focused on Janney. She could feel his scrutiny. "What are your plans for today, this week?"

Janney sat back, she was going to take her time, "I am meeting Mike Fallon today. We are going to visit the Back Door where Brian worked. He wants me to introduce him to the manager. I thought I'd check in on Derek Ball. Has he come in yet?"

"I do not think he has," Malcolm paused. "Look, for the time being, keep Derek out of the loop on the murder and LSD information. Do not discuss any of it with anyone. Answering a single question just leads to the next question. At some point you have to say 'no comment' so say it at the start. Once the full story breaks, you may get stopped in the street. If you find Derek, tell him to come see me or call me from home. When are you meeting Fallon?"

"I am not sure. He is going to call me today. We are going to have something to eat first."

Malcolm's eyes gave the impression he was processing something. "Mike Fallon is a good man, very intelligent, he has the facts, you can trust him. Listen, Janney, you are a very able person. You're very adaptable, more so than I think even you realise. I trust you and I know I can rely on you. I want you to keep your eyes and ears open. It's possible that some people are trying to ruin David's reputation and put him out of business, or at the very least reduce his business. There may be very dangerous people behind what happened on Saturday.

"If you hear of people blaming David for anything or suggesting breaking contact with him, don't say anything. Let me know of anything you hear. Remember what is said by others if you overhear a conversation. I want to know how this story is being shared. Let me know if you learn or remember anything relevant."

"The police will be in touch soon for a statement. The next few days will be difficult; let me know if you want to talk."

Janney smiled, "Thanks for that, I will keep you up to date. No interviews, right!" Without another word, Janney got up and left.

Work was going to be difficult to start. She decided she would just spend the day responding to some work problem, as and if it presented itself. She thought she would take it easy, she deserved to. She knew one thing, she had to find an empty room to sit in, no way could she sit down among the desks. She had to get away from prying eyes. It felt like a scene out of a bad horror film, any second now the eerie music would start.

# Chapter Fourteen

Once Janney walked past her desk, she saw there were a dozen or more messages piled up in her in-tray. She thought again one of these new answer phones might be a valid investment.

The messages had been left by people working within the open-plan area around her. People had clearly answered the telephone on her behalf, maybe just to stop it ringing or maybe just out of curiosity, given all that had happened.

Different people had received calls and been asked if they could drop a message onto Janney's desk. Janney read some of the messages, mostly 'Please Call Back.' Some messages had words or numbers written unclearly. She wondered if other messages had not been forwarded.

Maybe it was time to take up Malcolm's offer of an assistant or at least appoint someone to receive messages in her absence.

Janney saw that Derek Ball had not come to work. She decided to give him a call. She stood up and asked if anyone had his home telephone number. The reaction she received surprised her.

Some desks ignored her completely. One woman acted as though she must have been speaking to someone else.

Two others raised their heads and stared as if expecting her to repeat her question, so she did, slightly louder and clearer so that if anyone ignored her, they could be seen to be ignoring her.

'*Has all this to do with Saturday night?*' She wondered.

One man stood up. He was younger than Janney. She saw now they were all younger.

"Nope, can't help you." He was speaking as if for everyone, without even looking or asking. He then sat down without waiting for an answer. Janney thought of a few clever replies but for what point; their attitude was their biggest handicap.

Janney walked up two flights to the personnel department. After a series of misdirection's, she stood before a desk where she had been given an assurance, she should finally get all the information she requested.

"Can I please have Derek Ball's home telephone number?"

The situation again repeated itself. She was asked why she wanted it, then told that no one in the personnel department could give out a staff member's personal details or home number.

Views and opinions from several philosophical perspectives were exchanged, during which, the phrase 'jobs worth' kept being repeated.

Janney began to wonder how and when she started to have patience with such people. Somehow it crept into her behaviour without allowing her a chance to notice.

She telephoned Malcolm Offen, spoke for a moment, handed over the telephone to the personnel manager, who listened, she then stared hard at Janney.

The manager replaced the receiver, got up, returned and handed over Derek Bell's telephone number, all without a word. Then looked down and returned to her work.

Once Janney returned to her desk, the telephone rang, she picked it up and said, "Yes" with a bit more emphasis than she intended. It was Mike Fallon.

"Janney, I had almost given up on you being at work. I have been calling all morning."

"Really! Well, thanks for keeping the faith. It seems some people answered my phone, others didn't bother." Janney was past caring if people heard her conversation.

"I found somewhere we can eat; it has vegetarian food. It's close to the King's Head Pub, down the road from the Back Door. I will be in the pub at 6pm. You can come in anytime you like after that. We could then go for a meal and talk a bit, before going on to the club."

Janney felt a bit taken aback by this 'yes or no' approach. No one had ever tried it with her before. At the same time, she appreciated somewhere in the conversation she had been given a safe choice. She hated listening to people who only spoke to try and persuade her to do something.

"Yeah! That sounds good, no need to book a table then."

"I have never booked a table in my life. I don't understand that stuff. I like food well enough, but I hope clean tablecloths will never become an event for me. Do you like vegetarian? It doesn't have to be. I can find somewhere else."

"No! Veggie is good—you can't go wrong with veggie."

"OK! I will wait for you at the pub. Is there a good chance the manager will be at the Back Door?"

"I think it's very likely. I have always seen Finlay there on a Monday night. It's a music night."

"Great, I will wait for you in the King's Head. If anything comes up and you cannot make it, don't worry, I will go to the Back Door by myself. What's the manager's full name?"

"Finlay Bruce. He is very Scottish."

"OK! See you in the King's Head then."

"Fine, see you there."

Janney put the phone down. Once again, she felt everyone's eyes. It began to grate a little. She now knew people had just let her telephone ring.

She rang Derek Ball. After several rings, he answered. Once he heard Janney's voice, she could hear his relief.

"Janney, thank goodness! How are you?"

"I am fine. More to the point, how are you?"

"I am ok, have you seen the papers?"

"I have seen them. You're feeling better?"

"I am never going to feel better, but I am ok. I took the day off. Bit of a waste of time. The newspapers got my number."

"They might have mine. Did you meet Mike Fallon on Saturday?"

"No, who is he?"

"He is David Offen's lawyer. I am meeting him this evening. We are going to the Back Door. He wants to talk to Finlay Bruce. I think it might be good if you came."

"Why?"

"No real reason. I would like to see you; see how you are. We will be there about 9pm, maybe sooner. Try to come. Might be good to talk things through."

"Maybe I will; see how I feel. It will be good to get out of the house."

"Malcolm told me to tell you, that in no uncertain terms, are you to speak to anyone, absolutely no one about anything, seen or heard at the party. It's for the best, Derek, that for the time being, we all keep our mouths shut. The lid will blow soon enough. Malcolm also wants you to call him, if you're staying home."

"Is it urgent?"

"I think 'urgent' is taking on a whole new set of meanings."

"OK! I will speak with him tomorrow. I might be at the Back Door tonight. I will try. This Mike Fallon, is he alright?"

"Malcolm trusts him. I am going to give him a chance."

"Good enough."

"You're ok, eh?"

"Yeah."

"Good to hear your voice. Hope to see you. Take care."

Janney replaced the receiver. She thought for a moment, she was fed up with being a subject of curiosity. She picked up her messages and address book and stood up.

She spoke up again very clearly, for the whole room.

"Thank you, whoever you are, for taking and leaving these messages for me. I will do the same for all of you." Janney walked away. She had to find some privacy.

Maybe she could get some work done. Who was going to care anyway?

# Chapter Fifteen

Malcolm Offen left his office with plenty of time to visit 'Chief Inspector Hawkins.' He still could not get past calling him anything but 'Bill' or 'Hawkins.'

He had tried, for years, not to dwell on his wartime experiences. He knew there could never be any true empathy from others, in his heart he accepted why, he knew it would be impossible. He had tried for years to avoid thinking of those days but today perhaps that might change.

He caught a taxi, relaxed and started to watch the people in the streets. He saw the way the youth were changing, his first thought had been *'the same as they ever were,'* then suddenly there would be a burst of colour, new hairstyles and strange clothes for men and women.

*'Sign of a growing economy,'* he thought to himself, then laughed when he realised, *'I really am becoming middle-aged, looking at a haircut and thinking of the economy.'*

He wondered again about the real nature of empathy, if it were ever possible to connect with all the different attitudes of an emerging and diverse population. How is it possible to connect with the concerns of a new generation? or the interests any of the previous generations had for that matter?

Youth was becoming just a memory but was a connection with youth even necessary anyway? Why not just grow old, keep your health, your mental health, stay in touch with your own journey instead?

He made a weak attempt to convince himself once again that he was still almost as young as ever, or not so different than he had once been.

The people he worked with now seemed so different from the people he knew as a young man. Of course, everyone was focusing on different things then.

A week earlier, a long-haired protester had stopped Malcolm with a petition. Malcolm tried just for fun to engage him in an argument. Malcolm privately agreed with most of everything that was said, but the man suddenly stopped and told him, "You're refusing to be where you clearly seem to be."

Malcolm struggled with the statement for the next week, not really understanding it, annoyed at it, also thinking *'a bit more clarity from the speaker would have been useful,'* but sensing as well, it carried some sort of truth.

There had been occasions when Malcolm was accused, sometimes annoyingly so, by friends and family, of being afflicted with persistent honesty. It had never bothered him to hear that, it was none of their affair. Lately he found he had a growing desire, a need to be understood. His darkest thoughts were losing him connections with the people he most cared for.

He sat back in the taxi and confronted again the subject of age and changing times. He allowed himself the final admonition, *'May I please never start to impersonate the man I used to be?'*

"Maybe," he whispered, "it's now time to find better illusions."

Malcolm paid the taxi and walked into the same police reception area he had left the day before. He looked at the large wall clock.

*'That's the right way to fight time,'* he thought, *'buy a big clock.'*

He asked for Inspector Hawkins and sat on a plastic chair. Someone left a copy of a popular 'workers' socialist newspaper next to him. He always enjoyed reading these newspapers, especially if they reviewed the latest spy film.

Malcolm noted that his contemporaries would immediately, even before reading a word, always refer to the clear overriding left-wing bias within the articles.

He examined the writing style, which appeared quite good. It also referred, in turn, to the overriding right-wing bias within mainstream newspapers, especially those always proclaiming to be non-partisan, with their coverage.

*'How non-partisan can you be when you're silent on the complete facts?'* Malcolm thought.

"Non-partisan," he scoffed, "Just another myth. Silence itself shows an opinion." Malcolm composed himself, "Another one to add to my growing list of middle-class arguments."

An old memory returned—a French woman once sat down uninvited, to speak with Malcolm at a side cafe in Paris, the price being a coffee and a cigarette. She spoke good street English. She reflected on how Europe had so easily fallen for such stupid bigotry. She spoke of how normal it had all seemed at first, the reality of the bourgeois.

She spoke of how countries allowed repeated excuses or just made complaints when one political group began to dominate another group and how politicians in yet other countries only talked endlessly about it.

"It's not the opinions and attitudes, they change, they come and go. It is language. Language for all of us remains the prison. We are trapped within its limits to explain and convince, perhaps even to understand ourselves."

She slowly smoked her cigarette, as French women always seem to manage so easily. "People try to find answers in philosophy, but answers only exist within the scope of a limited narrative, a limited vocabulary. Language should be about meaning, not words, but we are unable to express every form of meaning, so we are bound by its words."

Malcolm watched the smoke surround her face as she leaned forward, "Limits in language seduce us into returning to the same questions, the ones we feel we can answer, the questions we decide to like and the answers we are bothered to examine. Power can silence popular dissent because of the limits within our language to identify our true complaint. We all do it to ourselves in the end."

Malcolm asked her, if that was the case, how then did she reach her opinions?

She threw her head back and gave a French shrug.

"Even if I do not say my own words, I make them mine."

Malcolm always remembered that half-hour conversation. Sometimes he wished he had bought the girl a second coffee. She might not then have asked for money, eventually cursing him and storming off.

# Chapter Sixteen

The Chief Inspector appeared, they both disappeared into an interview room.

"Glad you came, Malcolm. Have a seat."

"Happy to, Bill. I must admit I am genuinely glad you have done so well for yourself."

"You had a greater hand in that than you may know. Do you remember the final two weeks in Hamburg?"

The inspector pulled out his chair and sat down.

"We were both about to board that ship on a Friday and everyone was to be demobbed on the Monday, once we had docked at Southampton. You came to me and said you had to stay behind—do you remember?"

Malcolm shook his head, "I can't remember."

"You came to me and said there were 400 soldiers on the ship, only five sergeants, all the officers had been recalled."

"Yes! I remember now! there were going to be thousands of soldiers in Hamburg within days. All of them had to be sent home. Lots to do and organise. We had to get them onto ships quickly, there was little accommodation in Hamburg, precious few buildings left at all as I recall."

The Inspector remembered everything, he saw all the homeless children roaming the streets, he had been scared for them.

"Well anyway, you said regulations demanded that an officer had to accompany the 400 soldiers if they were travelling on a single ship transport. You gave me a commission to lieutenant, just for the trip, to last till I was demobbed the next week."

"That's right, I remember it all now."

"My discharge papers had me listed as a serving officer. A few months later I joined the police force. My application had me down as an ex-officer. Those two words carried a bit of weight. It allowed me a career."

"Surely not! You achieved your rank through hard work, ability and merit."

Hawkins paused, "Forgive me for saying so but that is a bit of a privileged cop-out. I achieved my rank through hard work and ability, but only because someone decided to recognise and reward the same, maybe give me an opportunity or two to shine. It was always going to be more important to keep the status quo intact. That's why my being seen as an ex-officer was important."

"Come on! We have both seen people rise through the ranks. It must be the same in the police force."

"Yeah! Some made it here and there. What difference does that make to the majority that were sidelined? I don't want to argue with you, Malcolm. You always gave respect to those who respected you."

"More to do with manners."

"It's a pointless argument," sighed Hawkins. "More to do with the way people are, instead of the system we were born into."

"Maybe! Maybe things will get better."

"Let's hope so. Even conversations like these are a bit of a cop-out. Resolutions made to satisfy us, for a future we have only a little hand in."

Malcolm looked hard at his old friend Bill Hawkins and knew he had not changed much. A little more articulate perhaps, but that's another sign of middle age—the arguments get repeated, additions made, statements become a bit more complete, people settle more inside themselves.

"Can I ask you, Bill, why the animosity towards my cousin?"

The inspector had to smile, "I am more inclined towards him now than I was at the house. When I had arrived, I was told three young girls were suffering the effects of some drug, LSD as it turned out. They had no knowledge of having taken it. I have a deep anger for anyone who would dope someone, especially youngsters, then laugh about it."

Malcolm spoke straight back with clear insistence, "My cousin never put anything in that punch bowl."

The inspector nodded, "I believe that now. There were glasses of punch lying around on different tables—several of the half-full glasses had the drug, but only those three girls were affected. Those who left their half-empty glasses on the tables were unaffected. The three affected took a glass of punch from the bowl a moment or so before Brian Nicholls fell. It's fair to assume the drug was dropped in the punch bowl and into several glasses on the tables just before the fall."

"I believe someone walked around dropping pills into the punch bowl and drinks on the table. Mr Nicholls' fall prevented a lot of people returning to the tables, finishing their drinks, it saved them from being affected."

The two sat in silence, Malcolm always regarded Bill Hawkins as a friend, he was still a friend, but he could see the man in front of him was the officer in charge. Malcolm felt the change, he was reporting to him now.

The Inspector began again. "I know someone had been in the attic with Brian Nicholls. The handle to open the windows had been wiped clean, as had the two handles on the attic door, Inside and out. Someone wiped them both before they left. There was dust everywhere. I brushed a lot of dust onto the floor outside the attic. I had seen a clear footprint with a marked heel inside the attic. I saw the footprints of you and your cousin, left by the attic door, once you both walked back down, you had both stepped onto my dust—no marked heel.

Malcolm had seen Bill Hawkins' personal strength of character many times when they both crossed Germany, he was reminded of it again as he watched him across the table.

The Inspector started speaking with more authority.

"Brian Nicholls had a lot more LSD in his system than anyone would ever take willingly. He came to the party to meet you but never spoke to you. Someone gave him LSD, maybe spiked him, probably gave him more after he was disoriented. Maybe within a drink, perhaps forced into him. I am proceeding with an assumption that whoever was in that attic came downstairs and dropped tablets of LSD into the punch bowl, as well the glasses. Unless, of course, more than one person was involved."

Malcolm thought again of the party. Everyone seemed so happy.

"LSD is not an illegal drug," said Malcolm.

"It should be, it will be soon, it's illegal if illegally manufactured. The drug is used by doctors for dealing with mental trauma or in some forms of therapy. I have seen dealers with bags of 100 or more tablets. it's not even expensive, a lot cheaper than cocaine."

"I do not think my cousin has ever used it."

"Malcolm, I am of the view that some people, people you might even know, may want to harm your cousin's business or reputation. Someone might have been paid, or even just asked for that matter, to place LSD into everyone's drink. Your cousin could have some strong enemies or dangerous competitors."

The inspector opened a pack of cigarettes. "A while ago I received information that a big concert your cousin was promoting had drugs delivered into the changing room. They were there alright, about five times more than anyone expected. We were not the only ones in that room surprised. The people we took away seemed genuinely confused. An informant later told me to visit your cousin on a given date as he would be offering drugs at a dinner party. Clearly, the purpose of the visit was to embarrass him with his guests."

Malcolm had formed similar conclusions himself. He had kept his silence because he knew his cousin would overreact. He was undecided as to the next steps to take, in truth he had no ideas.

The inspector lit his cigarette and relaxed into a conversation mode. He wanted to make some sense out of an environment he knew little about.

"Your cousin is very successful; to function, people need him as a friend or at least not an enemy."

"Applies to both of us."

"It would be better for some if he just disappeared. I have seen the way some businesses work. They approach the right people; they pay some money and say I want 'so and so' off the playing field. No violence please, no details! Just make it happen, do not contact us again, we do not want to be involved. We are respectable people."

The Inspector offered a cigarette. "Your cousin is in a business where people ruin lives, their own and others, all the while doing so in the public eye. I have heard idiots advocate drug use as a valid life choice. Some people seek out some sort of sense of detachment. A few have said it allows them a special truth, they even tried the old 'You just wouldn't understand argument'. A bit conceited if you ask me."

Malcolm had to laugh, he agreed with Bill, he had heard such conversations himself. In truth, at times he felt a complete disgust at such attitudes. He later knew, with hindsight, he was disgusted at himself for keeping silent, allowing such dangerous stupidity to be said out loud, to be said in his company, while in turn he offered no comment.

The Inspector became insistent again. "One thing all these pop stars demand is that others will always act to protect them. If they fail to get that, then they take their business and demand protection elsewhere. They do not care where the protection comes from, they want all they ever want, have success and fame and lead an unencumbered existence, no obligations, no responsibility."

Malcolm was unsure if the Inspector was talking to him now, or just getting feelings off his chest. The Inspector leaned back, he stared at the wall as if trying to find his own convictions.

"People stand in the wings untouched by all that occurs, acting through third or fourth parties, keeping their investments going, making their money; living their lives. If anything, bad happens, it's nothing to do with them. They had removed themselves, far away from the situation."

Hawkins stopped, turned back to his friend and had a short laugh, "Got on my soapbox there."

Malcolm smiled, "A man never declares his character so clearly as when he describes another man."

Bill Hawkins looked hard towards Malcolm,

"I remember you saying that a few times when we were in Germany. I thought it was a middle-class hogwash then, considering we were surrounded by Nazis. They described the nature of another man's character, they did it all the way through the war."

"You remember, we met people, respectable English people, happy to still agree with stuff like that, the same stuff all over again, just different people pointing different fingers."

Malcolm considered his old friend, "Bill, in all seriousness, you can't complain if people use drugs, for being who and what they are. A lot of people are weak and stupid, they make mistakes, we have both seen it. All sorts exist around us and will always be there."

Malcolm didn't want to argue further. He felt he better be careful. He had only just met an old friend. The years can change people. He had seen friends change till they became strangers.

Hawkins became more insistent. "People manipulate public perception, they use it for their own purposes, play on people's fear of change, it's a big fear. The newspapers have made a business playing on it."

The Inspector seemed to be releasing a very strong tension, he stood and arched his back.

"It changes the set down equations people want to live by. People really don't want to cope with that, when changes occur from what's expected, that's when the public reacts, things get nasty."

Hawkins relaxed the tension in his shoulders and pointed his finger. "What's more, I can very easily blame people for being who and what they are, as well as for what they do. I have been doing it for years. I get paid to do it."

They both laughed, The Inspector eased back in his chair. "When I thought your cousin had allowed those girls to be doped, I was 'this close.' Hawkins raised his thumb and forefinger together, *'this close,'* I was about to take him to the station in handcuffs. March him right past his precious guests, with his sleeves up. Shame the hell out of him. If I could have gotten away with it, I would have taken him all the way to the station in handcuffs on the top of a No 9 bus."

"To allow him a smoke," said Malcolm.

"I am not a monster."

"You have not changed, Bill. I remember when you needed men to load dead bodies onto lorries, you pulled six or seven German officers out of the prison compound."

Hawkins leaned forward and remembered, "You know they tried to argue with me, told me I must have made a mistake. They kept pointing at their badges. They pointed back at the ordinary soldiers. They could not believe that being an officer didn't matter anymore."

They both laughed, still comrades.

Hawkins took a breath, "I cannot investigate this matter without cooperation and information. I need an idea of the sort of people I am dealing with."

"These are people who will talk to you before they even listen to me. Will you help me out?

"Of course, Bill. If I even think someone is reluctant to talk or might be holding a secret, I will give you the name. My difficulty is I suspect my cousin's name is turning into mud. It looks like he might become a bit of a pariah."

"Yeah, I saw the papers, I can leave your cousin alone for now. I have still to interview everyone who was there, all we can hope for now is that someone will unintentionally reveal something or expose some sort of lead. I do not expect many people to assist our enquiries."

"I will get you whatever facts I can."

Hawkins stopped and considered Malcolm, "It took me a while to understand this little tidbit. You have probably heard the old saying, *'There is nothing so deceptive as an obvious fact'*. That the obvious allows each of us the opportunity to ignore a lot, that sort of thing."

Malcolm nodded, "They should teach that in schools."

"Well, when you're making enquiries, facts can become the enemy of truth. People can form opinions after learning a 'fact', they reinterpret the next thing they hear to allow them to believe all they prefer to be true, for all sorts of personal reasons, it exposes the values and attitudes we carry."

Malcolm nodded! "You can bend a narrative to support an assumption, false or otherwise, you then wind up prejudicing yourself. The army instructors taught me that. I haven't heard it said much since."

Hawkins burst out laughing, he looked incredulous, "You're saying officers walked around having already been told that! I can hardly believe it! It would have been useful if some of those idiots applied the idea once or twice, maybe even prevented a few punishments from being handed out. The Inspector stopped for a moment and shook his head at the memory.

"Well, it seems you're ahead of me, I just wanted to suggest you should try and keep your eyes and ears open for the full story. Now on a separate note, can you or your cousin give me or get me details of anyone you know of who deals or gives out LSD?"

"That might be a problem."

"I assumed as much, but I had to ask. So much for complete disclosure. No complaints, I wasn't expecting you to tell me,"

Malcolm and Bill Hawkins touched on a few different incidents which occurred during the party, the various individuals who might have left before the police arrived.

They eventually began to discuss what they had seen in Germany. They then left the subject alone, it was just a memory now, part of who they were, who they became. Both knew of each other's experience and felt a bit better. They each saw their personal isolation within the memories shift a little.

The two of them looked up together and saw the time. They agreed to keep in touch; both fully intended to. Malcolm walked into the reception area, much more at ease. He took another look at the big clock. *Must get one*, he thought.

# Chapter Seventeen

It was beginning to rain, just enough to notice. Janney had no umbrella, which she didn't care about normally, but today she did not want to get her hair wet. She knew why, this did annoy her.

She was rushing, on her way to meet Mike Fallon. She wanted to look good, but why should she rush anyway or even care if her hair looked wet? All of it was making her increasingly irritated.

She had not met a guy in a pub for a drink for more than a year. She had told herself this meeting was just to discuss the events of Saturday, to bring Mike to the Back Door to meet the manager. *'Why are we having a meal anyway? How did I get talked into this? There is a lot of confusion here. I didn't cause it.'* "No!" She said firmly, "I am not going to hurry." Then she had to step inside a doorway as the rain started coming down heavily.

As she caught her breath in the doorway, she knew something changed by her just thinking about guys again.

If she cared to consider it, she knew she had baggage. Some dreams kept returning, echoes of her mother sitting across a table, waiting for her to say something, refer to an awful experience that had haunted her for years.

Her mother had told her, "Time does not always heal, but it does give space to learn to cope. Everyone has fears. You don't have to control your fears, you just stop them from controlling you."

In the last few years, with the trust Malcolm had shown, her slowly gaining confidence, the unexpected career and having a little travel, things had begun to knit together. *'Maybe I have stepped onto a new learning curve? That would be nice. Maybe I am ready,'* she thought. *'Ready to try for new answers to old questions, maybe even new questions.'*

The rain slowed down. Janney stepped out and called a taxi.

Mike Fallon had mentioned to David Offen about meeting Janney. David was pleased. Mike noticed this because it was clear David was walking around looking more and more pleased with himself.

David was wary each time he started a new conversation with Mike. He always anticipated Mike would try to spin his head with his latest stolen epigrams, each one of them coming out of the bottom of who knows where.

David was however very ready to talk if the subject could be women. Something he had never discussed with Mike, but which might now and for a first time allow for a little common ground.

What David was now also discovering, which he realised with delight, was that Mike had little to say on the subject. In fact, he was appearing a bit shy and reticent.

"I have never heard you speak of knowing any women, Mike, much less going for a drink with one."

"Well! I don't bandy around women's names."

"Quite right! Quite right." This was too much for David, for the first time with Mike, he felt he held the upper hand.

"You know, the King's Head is not a very trendy pub. I could find you a better watering hole if you like."

"No thanks, it's all arranged, anyway, maybe soon it will be 'discovered', you can bring all your socialite girlfriends there."

*'Oh, good grief! This is golden, he is becoming defensive.'*

"Mike, don't be like that; I think you and Janney are a good match."

Mike spun around. He moved as if he was going to say something forcefully. David stood still. *'Wow! Finally, he is coming out of his shell.'* Mike then stood back, relaxed a bit, he was taking a breath.

"David," Mike spoke slowly, "I hardly know Janney, I don't know her at all. Please listen to what I am saying carefully if you want us to stay friends."

Mike stood square in front of David with his palms raised. "I will never have these sorts of conversations, not with you, not with anyone." There was a pause. "I have a serious line here. Please do not cross it."

David raised his own hands to his chest, palms out. He also took a step back. David had seen it; he had accepted it.

*'Well, well,'* he thought.

Mike enjoyed David's company most of the time. He even enjoyed annoying David, mainly because he felt David truly wrestled with new ideas if they confused him.

At the same time David would adopt a pose that if he had not understood the subject matter, it was only because he had never really cared about it anyway.

Mike's secret truth was that he had a talent for making observations and then identifying them on the spot with other associations, much as a quick comedian could do.

He coupled this with a beginner's knowledge of philosophy and enough Zen references to fill a trivia book. It had been a technique he employed for years. It helped him in conversations when people cornered him. He was amazed every time his gobbledygook impressed people.

Mike decided early; when only a teenager, people understood what they were told only as far as they cared to understand, and if so, then only if it was at a convenient moment.

It assisted matters if you threw in something which complemented their set views or values or if it matched up with their personal interests or curiosity. That always helped any understanding.

He once watched a very old relative, trying to make sense of thoughts and memories, muttering to himself, "You cannot hold the same piece of water twice."

Mike had touched, barely once or twice, the ephemeral nature of his own true deep-held beliefs and sense of true self. He knew how the grasp of that moment could last an instant and then drift away through the fingers. He also knew if he ever visited that place again, it could all be different. He would be different.

When Mike met with David, he enjoyed offering new water for David to grab at, making sure not to be too boring while doing it.

Janney eventually got to the King's Head at 6.15 pm. The pub was empty. She saw Mike in the corner playing pinball. She walked over to a table and sat down.

Mike smiled. "Be with you in a minute." It was three minutes later before Mike walked over to Janney and asked what she wanted. He returned with their drinks.

"Sorry to keep you waiting. I was about to beat the top score."

*'No real answer to that,'* thought Janney, feeling a bit annoyed at being expected to sit alone in a pub. "Good job this place is empty," she said a little louder than intended.

Mike seemed to ignore the remark. "So! Malcolm has brought you up to date?"

"Yes," said Janney. "You got any ideas?"

"About what?"

"About what to do next." Janney was starting to get a little more irritated, *'He asked me to come here, if I have to be the lead in this conversation, he can go and play some more pinball.'*

Mike appeared to be in a great mood. "At this moment in time, I am just fishing around. Not being a real detective, it's hard to know where to begin. The only real point of inquiry we have is Brian Nicholls. We can probe around there."

Janney took a silent breath, *'OK! If he wants everything to be all business, then fine.'*

"I may have got Derek Ball to turn up tonight."

"Sorry! Remind me."

"Brian was Derek Ball's guest, his plus one, on Saturday."

"Oh! Right! I remember now. Excellent!"

There was a bit of an uncomfortable silence. Mike appeared to Janney as if he was just trying to look for a subject to begin talking on. This seemed to Janney a bit strange, given that they clearly had a lot to talk about.

Janney decided to break the silence. She smiled, "Sometimes the best way to start a conversation is to say the wrong thing."

Mike smiled back, "I have a reputation for doing that."

Janney stared into her drink, "What's your view on LSD?"

Mike had already told Malcolm and David his position on LSD. He wanted no arguments on the subject. He hoped Malcolm had already told Janney his views.

"That sort of stuff terrifies me."

"Some people have found it helps them."

Mike sipped his drink and gave it some thought.

"Maybe! But that has been said about a lot of things. It's not always true. It can be a bit of a fallback excuse for a bad decision."

Mike clearly had a convinced view. "I do not believe in even recreational drugs being a good idea. Some people surrender a lot of time to them. Their best time. They are not a communal thing despite what people say. They seem, to me, ultimately a selfish practice. Then again, how far can I judge, if I have already made my mind up?"

Janney lifted her glass. "You believe everything in moderation then, like drink."

"Some things I do not want to try at all. When my demons visit me, I want to be able to tell them to leave, take their names, wave them goodbye."

"Have you got a lot of demons?"

"Who knows, what's a lot? Demons are personal, they come and go, they grow and shrink, when you're alone and when you're with company." Mike raised his glass, "No demons here tonight, though."

"Good to know," said Janney.

Mike and Janney talked some more about the newspapers. They agreed the story was being manipulated. Someone was clearly out to get David Offen.

They talked about current music, the music at the Back Door that evening, the music they liked, the music Brian played.

Janney touched again on the idea that the whole situation had a root in someone wishing harm to David's business. The more she thought about it, it made sense, she saw that a whole range of people would now be very happy by all that occurred. The business had nasty characters. She had seen people beloved by the public who made her skin crawl.

Mike had guessed the same thing. From what he had witnessed, some artists, the music groups especially, were constantly surrounded by new deal makers. Their managers had a constant paranoia that their signings were about to go elsewhere.

Eventually, the conversation wore itself out. They both got up, it was time to eat.

As they passed the pinball machine, Mike showed Janney how the scores could be made. He showed her his top score on the machine.

He put in a coin and Janney played her first-ever game of pinball. The two competed. They both laughed and Janney thoroughly enjoyed it. It was now off her list of 'things to do.' She told Mike it was also on her list of "things I never need to do again."

# Chapter Eighteen

David and Malcolm were sitting silently in Malcolm's house. They watched the news on the television. There seemed to be nothing of immediate interest.

David spoke first, "I contacted a few people today, about projects in the pipeline for weeks. They cut me short and said they would get back to me."

Malcolm finished his drink, "Give me their names. I will ask around, see what's being said." Malcolm stared at the wall. He had a palpable urge to act. He sat upright.

"Whoever put the LSD in the punch bowl wanted to do you harm. We can work with the assumption that it was the same person who hurt Brian. The two events were close together. Could these have been two independent actions? No! I still think it was a single person. Maybe there were two motives? Who would want to upstage you, hurt you?"

"I have wracked my brain, Malcolm. I cannot think of anyone who was there. There were businesspeople at the party but no one who would immediately benefit."

"No!" said Malcolm, "There are different considerations here. If it was just someone trying to take business from you, they would have no reason to involve Brian. A lot of time was spent on that; it must have had its own purpose."

Malcolm paced the floor. "When Brian fell, no one continued drinking or went to the punch bowl. The drug was put in the bowl only moments before. Three drank from it, then Brian fell. Brian's death stopped others' drinking; his death was probably not intentional; it may have even ruined a set plan."

David stared at Malcolm, "When did you work that out, talking with Hawkins?"

"No! Maybe! Sometimes when you just say your thoughts out loud, they can lead you up the garden path. Try doing it, you can surprise yourself with new ideas and find out they are your own ideas."

David sank into his chair. "Perhaps no one hates me, maybe putting the drug in the bowl was just generally malicious, No! Someone would have to hate me to do that."

Malcolm saw there could be variations in motives. He remembered Hawkins' advice against fixating on a single fact or a single interpretation of a fact.

"Maybe this was meant as an attack on another guest or group of guests."

"That still leaves Brian," said David.

"He wanted to see me. Why? It might explain a lot."

David walked to the wall, "Maybe we are avoiding seeing something we really do not want to observe."

Malcolm had to laugh, "Curse of the ruling classes that. Bit of a family bag of worms you may never want to open."

"By the time we notice who is trying to take business away, the damage will be already done. Let's face it, the damage has already been done."

Malcolm paced the floor. "Some people think that a dose of LSD is a good thing, everyone should try it. Do you know anyone like that?"

David shook his head, "I tend to ignore people when they talk like that. No one I saw at the party, but then we didn't know everyone."

David was filled with contempt. "You find headcases everywhere. We might have to deal with them, but you don't need them as friends."

Malcolm thought back to Hawkins and all he had said about people who just stand by and watch.

"Some people take that drug and can become very deluded. They can change. They could have thought the punch bowl or glasses were a laugh. The whole thing could have been on a spur of the moment, an impulse thing."

David put his head in his hands. "We are getting absolutely nowhere."

"We are looking for a trail, assuming there is one to find. Maybe the whole thing was not planned or only partially planned. Everything we come up with will be just guesswork."

Malcolm put his hand on his cousin's shoulder. "We are not going to come out of this untouched. Take time to remember how lucky we have been. Maybe this ride is just ending—we might have to look for a new one."

Malcolm had to laugh again. "Could have been worse—we might have drunk some of the doctored punch."

David smiled, "Not something you want to do before you're questioned by police."

"Might have prevented us impressing the constabulary with our elite patrician style, David."

Both were silent.

"Poor guy," said Malcolm, remembering Brian.

"Yeah," said David

# Chapter Nineteen

Janney had not known what to expect when she and Mike left the King's Head. They both walked towards the Back Door when Mike stopped short; Janney found herself in front of a Pizza Parlour.

Janney looked inside and saw a few empty tables, with chessboard tablecloths. Her immediate thought, her only thought, was a quick disappointment.

"Why be surprised?" She sighed. She could see somehow that a Pizza Parlour was going to be consistent with the style of this guy she was out with.

*'Not at all what I was hoping for,'* she thought as they entered the mostly empty restaurant. *'Perhaps I should tell him I do not like pizza.'*

"Do you like pizza?" Mike asked.

Janney grimaced, "I tried a frozen pizza once, got it from one of those new supermarkets. I did not care for it."

"We can go somewhere else if you like, but there is nothing frozen from a supermarket here. This is the real deal."

Janney saw a man behind the counter, throwing and spinning around a circular pastry in the air, then placing it into an overhead oven. She had never seen that done.

Mike was smiling, "It's nothing like what you get in the supermarket. I would really enjoy being the one to introduce you to the authentic stuff."

Despite her misgivings, Janney found herself enjoying Mike's enthusiasm for her to have a new experience.

"Do you know anything about wine?" Mike asked. They discovered neither of them knew anything about wine, so agreed on the house red. They read the menu on the possible different toppings. There were a lot of combination choices, again a new idea for Janney.

Janney looked through the menu. She asked, "What sort of cheese are they offering here, where it says cheese?"

Mike's face was covered by his menu. "I don't know. Maybe they don't know."

Mike smiled behind the menu, "It occurs to me that throughout the ages, all the great philosophers and poets have been conspicuously silent on the subject of cheese."

*'This guy is a great talker,'* thought Janney. *'Wait a minute, that sounded comfortable. I bet he has been out with girls and repeated that line a few times before.'*

"You will have to forgive me—I did not go to university. I do not know any philosophers or poets. I suspect my teachers at school didn't know any either."

Mike appeared a little embarrassed. "Sorry! Sometimes I say stuff to appear clever. Appearing clever can get in the way of being so. There, you see, I did it again."

Janney had no intention of knocking trite phrases back and forth. "I never read all the books that would allow me to repeat quotations or to be so frightfully amusing."

Janney could not help but just watch Mike, "I am curious as to why your conversation dances around so much. You appear nervous?"

Mike lowered his menu, "Curiosity killed the cat. I got the job of interviewing the witnesses."

"You're doing it again." Janney dropped her menu onto the table, speaking clearly as if willing him to stop.

Mike held his hand up. "OK! OK! You're calling me out. Believe me, I do appreciate it!"

Mike took a few seconds to pause, "For the last couple of years, probably longer, all I have had in my life has been work. The people I deal with do not want advice on what they can or cannot do. They want me to tell them how they can get away with doing all they want to do."

Mike felt inside this conversation might be an opportunity to stop playing games for a while, take a real chance and step out from behind himself.

"Do you think people care about or even understand half of what they hear other people say? I am not used to people being that interested in the stuff I come out with. Clever statements help close conversations when people are not even listening to each other. You play this sort of game for a while; it becomes a style of talking."

Janney had never been impressed with bare-faced honesty, or long excuses for behaviour, especially from someone she hardly knew. A part of her wondered if this was just another part of the same game. She wasn't interested in playing games.

Her thoughts still carried the voice of her mother and all she said about trusting people. Inside she felt she wanted the guy sitting in front of her to be genuine.

"How about we leave the games behind, we try listening to each other? Janney waited for an answer.

Mike studied Janney. His eyes widened. "I think I would genuinely enjoy that." Mike paused. "But first, have you picked your toppings?"

Janney and Mike settled on the toppings for their pizza. They both went to the counter and watched it being made.

Janney did not want to reveal much of her background. She had tried revealing her history to educated people before and then seen the dynamics shift. She wanted a parity between herself and Mike.

Mike did not talk about his work or clients again. Somehow the subject matter gravitated towards education.

"I saw people at university who were there only because it was seen as a normal thing to do, as if it was expected of them."

"Not the case for you, then," said Janney.

"I was going to need a job once I got out. I like the law anyhow. I like the stories."

"What do you mean?"

"The law is a series of stories, put together as part of a big picture that everyone agrees to like. The colours keep changing, everyone's taste in the colour's change."

Janney decided to test him, "My mother used to tell me that under English law, you're innocent until proven to be Irish."

Mike half nodded, "The law and justice are friendly cousins, but sometimes they are not on speaking terms."

Mike took a bite of Pizza. "The big difference between stupidity and intelligence is that there is a limit to people's intelligence."

Mike put his slice of pizza down, "This is where I start drifting into being a clever feller again. How did we get away from you?"

"I have always been here." Janney was enjoying the pizza. She was glad she had experienced something new, something she now knew she would try again.

Janney decided she could reveal a little. "I think I would have liked a better education. Not sure what I would have wanted to study though. I would like to know how to argue my thoughts."

Mike finished his pizza. "Arguments can be a bit overrated. When you sit with lawyers, all anyone tries to do is defend their corner. In law, the argument is nothing, leverage is everything."

Janney wanted her point properly appreciated. "I have met a lot of very educated people. I thought quite a few were idiots. Most of them didn't even care to appear otherwise."

"It would be nice to be confident with what you know, to know your opinions have been fully worked out, that they stand alone. Credible, you people call it. I don't like being cautious when I say what I think.

Mike had to smile, "You mean you want to consider and understand the full ramifications of what you say, the true intention, the background, behind your viewpoint, before you even start to say it out loud, you might be a Renaissance woman. Janney."

Janney just sighed "I would like it if we stayed on the same page, I don't want to have to ask what you mean by that. Conversations do not have to be a competition."

Mike looked at Janney, he paused, he knew whatever he said next, he had to show something. He spoke slowly, "I have no wish to compete with you." He wanted her to believe him.

Milk allowed a few more seconds. "People accumulate knowledge and opinions but when it comes to time to speak aloud, it will never be the same as it was in their heads. The voice in your head is rarely the same as the one that comes out of your mouth."

Janney thought about that. "Sounds like a good habit."

Mike was stopped short. That answer surprised him, it required some thought. "You're a careful woman, Janney, each of us tries to explain our behaviour, our thoughts, though much of it remains mysterious to us. Behaviour and motives will change for all of us, for some reason we are taught or compelled to then offer other people the reasons why."

Janney could follow the point. "Instead of looking for why, you could accept change as natural or normal in the course of experience, of how your life is working out."

She began to explore the thought; this was a conversation she never expected. "As far as explaining ourselves is concerned, I have always seen that as a bit of an indulgence, but I accept we all like indulgences. Do you think someone in the west of Ireland picking stones and potatoes out of a field for twenty years feels a need to explain his motives to anyone, even to himself?"

Janney was thinking hard. "Understanding your motives might not work well, it depends on your capacity to cope with what you discover, whether it satisfies you or keeps you from ever being content with your lot, whatever that means."

Mike studied Janney; he saw he had to respect the space she was making for herself. "You are diving in deep with those thoughts, Janney, they are not easy to answer."

Mike laughed again. "I have met people educated far beyond their own intelligence. I am not trying to be funny there, I truly believe that. You're confident enough, Janney. You have people who like your company and want your advice. That's only because of who you have shown yourself to be, not because of your views or motives. There are people happy to stand beside you if you need help. A lot of people never know that."

Janney felt the silence, "I get a lot of anxiety sometimes."

"You appear gutsy to me, Janney. Can I say something about anxiety? I realise you would have already considered all the parts to it; it's part of your own journey; it must be very private."

"Go ahead."

Mike gave Janney his full focus. "Anxiety goes away, at least for a while. It will not always be there. The way you tell yourself your own story matters; unfortunately, anxiety can give little things a big shadow."

"Your mind will answer most questions if you can learn to wait for the answer. Never imagine you're permanently trapped by anxiety. Never imagine you're helpless or you're a victim. You have treasures within you that are infinitely greater than any the world has to offer."

"Thanks, Mike."

They finished the pizza; talked about the menu again and then left to walk to the Back Door.

As they walked, she laughed quietly to herself. She knew Mike would have stolen much of what he said from other people, from some book. It didn't matter, it was still nice to listen to. She liked his conversation. It showed the stuff he listened to. He listened to her as well. What was it her mother told her,

*"They talk of ideas they never use, Ideas they just repeat from other conversations."*

As she watched the pavement, she realised that if she ever felt intimidated by Mike's education or intelligence, she could always carry the thought of him getting all excited trying to reach a high score at pinball. She noticed she beat his top score at pinball, and it didn't seem to bother him.

# Chapter Twenty

As Mike and Janney approached the Back Door, they could see a crowd outside trying very hard to get in.

"Looks busy," said Mike.

"On a Monday night too," Janney was surprised as the band that evening was not particularly good, or even well known.

There were two very large imposing doormen, both with big smiling faces, who were giving preferential attention to a crowd of girls, all smiling back at the doormen and trying not to have to pay the five shillings entrance fee. The doormen kept laughing, they gave each girl a little stamp on the back of their hands and let them pass.

Mark turned to Janney, "Is there any way to get through the crowd? Do the doormen know you?"

Janney shook her head, "Not these guys." Suddenly she saw Finlay Bruce, walking up and down, assessing the crowd. "Finlay!" shouted Janney, they both walked over.

"Hello, Janney, I did not expect to see you tonight."

"Finlay, this is Mike. You're the reason we are here. Would it be possible to talk?"

Finlay shook Mike's hand.

Mike was quick to tell Finlay that he was acting for David and Malcolm Offen. He began apologising for cornering him in the street, given how busy he seemed to be.

"Not as busy as you may think. I have three managers running things on a music night. I just like to see how things are working outside. We have a new scheme—we first let groups of girls in free. The place soon fills up after that."

Finlay Bruce had a strong Scottish accent, but every word was enunciated perfectly.

"What can I do for you, Mike?" Finlay spoke as he continued to face the crowd.

"I am looking for some background details about Brian Nicholls. Anything you can say or tell us? It may be the case, of course, that you have nothing to say. We would just appreciate the opportunity to just talk, whenever you have a free moment."

Finlay turned to Janney, "Your friend certainly has some manners, eh! Janney?"

Janney smiled. "He has a lot of something, that's for sure."

"This place will be full in a half hour or so. Ask for me at the bar. We will go somewhere and talk."

Finlay beckoned Mike and Janney up to the security standing at the door. They both got their wrists stamped and went in.

Once inside, Mike quickly saw seats were at a premium. The band had not started but it was already almost too loud to talk. Mike looked left and right. "Do you want to stand here and watch the band, jump about a bit on the spot?"

"Not right now," said Janney, straight-faced, determined not to be outdone. "Maybe later, thanks for asking. They have great peanuts here."

Mike saw two seats on a bench against the wall. He moved to claim them. "Stay here. Do not give my seat away to anyone else. I will try and get us both a beer."

After returning with the drinks and some peanuts, it was clear a conversation was going to be impossible. The noise made it difficult to even think of anything to say.

Any free seat was grabbed quickly, the floor was now filled with different groups. Guys trying to decide which girls to approach, groups of girls looking over their shoulders at crowds of boys, some little crowds laughing, happy in their own company. Mike and Janney didn't speak, but both would have agreed, no one was there for the music.

The band began playing. The sound was uneven. The balance between the speakers was wrong. The drum and bass sound made it difficult for anyone to concentrate.

Mike looked towards the bar, at the opposite end of the hall, far away from the stage, well away from the speakers. It had to be the best place to stand. Once the band got into full swing, Mike and Janney knew without asking, they could not continue sitting where they were.

Mike pointed at the bar. They pushed their way up to the bar and rested on the mahogany. They saw drinks on the counter bouncing inside the glasses along with the bass sound. All they could do now was wait for Finlay Bruce.

It was an uncomfortable hour before Finlay appeared. He saw them both and led them to a room behind the bar. Once the door was closed, the sound subsided, but the base vibrations were still resonating into the door and walls.

"Sorry to keep you waiting. I wanted to get all the business out of the way so we could talk uninterrupted." Finlay appeared in a jovial mood; business was not one of his problems.

"At this point in the evening, I can retreat a bit." He looked at Mike and waved at the door. "It can be a bit much, eh!"

Janney had been to the Back Door before. She had seen other venues, some better, many worse. She had known what to expect. Mike appeared as if he had trouble trying to mentally function.

"Do you mind if I take a minute to recover, Mr Bruce?"

Finlay laughed, "Call me Finlay."

Mike turned to Janney and said in a slow but truly bewildered tone, "Do people really want to go through all that, just for the idea they might have a good time?"

"To try and meet people they can't listen to, It's like some sort of endurance test."

Finlay laughed again, "There are tricks to it, you need to know where the speakers are, best spots to stand in. It helps if you like the music. I don't think I will have this lot back though, they're no good. Here, come with me, let me take you somewhere better."

He led them out again into the noise. They walked along the back of the bar, onto the other side of the hall, they then turned towards a staircase.

They walked down the stairs to the corridor which ran underneath the bar, then to a big door. It was covered in an iron wool foam. Once the door was closed behind them, Finlay turned on the light. Mike took a breath; they were finally standing in complete silence.

# Chapter Twenty-One

Mike looked around the room. "I don't think I will take peace and quiet for granted again."

Mike saw a large drum kit behind some screens, several microphones stands and three large reel-to-reel recording machines. By the far wall, there was what Milke assumed was a recording, mixing desk, with dials and switches and monitors. On the floor, there were several silver metal cases.

Finlay went to the wall and set up some folding chairs by a small table. He then went behind the recording desk and brought back a bottle of whisky and some paper cups.

"So, you're here about Brian. First, what can you tell me about what happened?"

Janney spoke first. She, Brian and Finlay had known each other. She accepted Finlay was entitled to hear what some of what happened. She spoke of the night and all she saw but gave no information other than what was public knowledge. He fell from a window, no evidence it was a jump, no clear motive and no message left.

All information about the LSD, that Brian was affected by it, that it was found in glasses and the punch bowl and that others drank it, that was still private information.

Janney still had a clear vision of Malcolm warning her in his office. Finlay Bruce could easily see secrets were being kept.

"The newspapers have more to say than you two."

Mike spoke over Janney, "The newspapers have made guesses, which came from third-party accounts, from people who know little. Put no faith in what the newspapers say."

"I do not need to be told that." Finlay directed his attention squarely at Mike. "Listen, I have not just got off the bus. There is more to be said here."

Finlay poured another drink for himself and Mike and waited for them both to speak. He swallowed his drink and after seeing the silence continue, he finally spoke.

"I would like to know a bit more. Brian was a good worker, he did me a few good turns and was a wee bit of a friend of mine. I feel a little invested here."

Mike decided to go for broke, "The police have told us a lot more than has been disclosed. They asked for it to be kept quiet. They are making enquiries; it would help them if they discovered who knows what without first being told."

"Everything is going to come out, probably within the week. There are no secrets, no conspiracy, no cover-up."

Janney added "If you help us, it could help us get to the truth a little faster."

Finlay Bruce searched both sets of eyes. It went against everything he had ever been taught, to give up something for nothing, especially when he thought he was being manipulated, that secrets were being kept.

He could see nothing was going to be volunteered from the two sitting opposite. Why should he offer anything? He owed them nothing.

A part of him was tempted to say *"to blazes with both of you"* but he decided if the conversation continued, he might hear a little bit more. Who knows, maybe he could do poor Brian a service.

He knew Janney a little bit, he liked her; perhaps she carried a genuine motive. This other guy, he pegged as very different, one to keep watching.

"What is it you want to know?" Finlay said slowly.

Mike spoke again. He saw Finlay was going to speak only on his own terms. "First of all, can you tell us anything about Brian? Anything you noticed recently that was different, anything that had changed, anything he said that you remember, worthy of note."

Finlay still had not made up his mind about the man sitting across from him. He had hardly touched his second whisky, which Finlay noted marked him as a careful man.

"You know the police came this morning and asked similar questions. A couple of ordinary constables, just taking names really, jotting stuff down with their pencil into their little black book."

"They said someone would come and interview me in a day or so, might ask for a statement. Maybe I should wait for that."

"How about we just have a conversation instead?" Janney said.

Finlay laughed. His laugh showed clear evidence of a Scottish highland background.

"A conversation, you say? Now that sounds nice. What is it you're going to offer in this conversation, other than questions? Can I ask questions in this conversation?" There was a marked silence, Finlay's smile had changed.

Janney saw she had to find common ground. "Finlay, there is a lot of new information. I promised my boss to keep a lid on it—the story will break soon enough. I cannot break my word. When the story comes out, the next day, I will be here and lay it all out for you, answer all your questions."

Finlay paused. He felt Janney was doing her best. He knew her livelihood possibly rested on anything she said and whatever she did. He had to respect that. He had been in such situations himself, more than once.

Finlay put his drink down and laid his hands across his stomach.

"Brian had no family to speak of. He told me once he had been in a children's home, foster parents for a while. He had an early talent for the piano, which was just as well. He had no talent for talking to people, no girlfriends that I ever saw, which is a pity. I think if he had one, it would have done him a power of good. I do not know the medical term for it, but Brian had a personality problem. You could see it sometimes when he spoke. There were words for it where I grew up. Disgusting words."

Finlay poured another drink for himself. "He told me that he spent all day on the piano growing up. Later he became very good with the flute. Someone helped him get into some sort of music school or college."

Finlay lifted his drink. "He really did know his stuff, could write it all down. He did a lot of work with the bands that come in here. Everyone liked him."

Mike looked around the room. He stood and walked towards the boxes; he looked down on them. "What sort of things happen down here?"

Finlay pointed around the room. "We have bands that come down here to record and experiment. You write a song, maybe on a guitar or piano, you sit around with other musicians. By the time it's finished, it's not much like the same song. That lot upstairs will not be coming down, I doubt I will have them back."

"They can make demonstration tapes that they send off to the record company, maybe sell themselves or the song, get a contract. Put audition stuff together for promoters, try to get on a concert bill as a support act."

Mike knew he was out of his depth. He could not think of an appropriate question.

Janney tried to push matters forward. "Who did Brian come down here with?"

"Everybody," said Finlay. "Anyone who asked him. He would have slept down here if he could. Some bands come back regularly, play upstairs regularly; they come down at the end of the night, sometimes with food and drink, maybe pull an all-nighter. My managers have opened in the morning and have had to kick them out. Brian would have been with them all night, playing away."

Mike tried to gather his thoughts; he could see that Finlay was not playing. He was the sort of man he appeared to be, whoever that was.

The best way to deal with him was to relax into oneself, take your time, much like the Scotsman was already doing.

"When the bands record here, do they make use of this?" Mike pointed at the mixing desk.

"Oh yes! They make a big use of that. It's easy to use but difficult to master. Sometimes they bring someone in with experience of using it."

"Could Brian use it?"

"I think he could, a bit, enough to make a demo tape."

"These are all the tapes?" Mike pointed down at one pile of boxes within an open case on the floor.

Finlay got out of his chair. "Yes, and no." He went to one of the larger metal cases, opened it and there were 20 to 30 open cardboard boxes. "You have these tapes for just rehearsing, to play back, see how everything sounds." He opened the next box. There were a dozen or so sealed cardboard boxes.

"These are larger, better-quality tapes, better sound, used for the final demo, the ones you record on, then take away to play for others. Lot more expensive."

Mike pointed at the first box. "So, these tapes are used and left here."

Finlay opened all the boxes and left them open. "Yes, they use them and then tape back over them again." Finlay showed Mike the label on the lid of one box. There were dates and names of bands which had been crossed off and a most recent date written underneath.

"If you record on the thicker higher quality tapes, you pay for them and take them away. They are used once; they cannot get reused."

"Do you mind if I look at all these for a few minutes?" Mike said.

"Go right away."

Mike began taking all the unsealed boxes out of the metal cases. He put them in different piles, with the different names on the labels. He moved them around into date order. Janney and Finlay watched, wondering what he was doing.

Janney took Finlay aside and told him quietly, "Thanks. Finlay, I appreciate your help. I want you to know we will get to the bottom of this and you're going to be part of it. I promise I will keep you up to date with everything."

Finlay kept a straight face but smiled inside. He had done little more than just explore his own curiosity. He wasn't sure he liked being thanked by someone when in truth he had not even tried to offer help. He enjoyed listening to Janney, though. He thought she was a fine girl, as far as one could know an acquaintance.

He was still suspicious of Mike. He did not entirely recognise the man. He reminded him slightly of the pawnbroker he watched as a child, walking the streets in his hometown. Somebody who was often called upon, but who never received a smile or a greeting in public.

Mike made two piles of tapes from the opened boxes.

"Finlay! Can I take these? I will pay you for them or bring you replacement tapes, new ones, tomorrow."

"What! Why on earth would you want these? What's going on? What are you playing at?"

Mike counted the boxes. "Could be nothing, just a shot in the dark. How much for the lot?"

"Sorry," said Finlay, "I need these tapes. What use are they to you anyway?"

"You said it yourself," said Mike. "These tapes get taped over. Some have been taped over a few times, I promise I will get you new ones tomorrow. I can leave you these two; they were used last weekend."

Finlay's mind was moving quickly, he knew there was a newer, better range of tapes in the shops now.

He was confident if these two said they would return then they would be back. He just felt worried he might be missing something important. Maybe it was nothing; the tapes just might just be more important to them than to him.

"Done! I want you back tomorrow. Now listen, I really do not want to have to ask about you."

Mike smiled, "No worries, I know I do not want to get on your wrong side. I might never find the way back."

Finlay was finally convinced. He was never going to trust this man; he was too quick with a reply.

'*A real talker*,' thought Finlay. He studied Mike again, "Let me get some ribbon and we can tie these together."

The two men agreed on the number of tapes to be delivered, the time for delivery, the brand name and the specialist shop where to buy them.

Finlay refused Mike's card with his address and telephone number. He said he trusted Mike completely. He knew with a grim certainty that if he wanted to find this man again, he was not going to use a card.

They carried the boxes upstairs. The crowd had rushed to the bar to get new drinks before the last call. Janney stopped and thanked Finlay again. It was getting a little bit too much for Finlay. He kept telling her it was all ok.

The two men carried the two piles of boxes, each tied up with ribbon, out to the front door.

Janney saw Derek at the bar and called him over. She asked if he could get them all a taxi. "Where to?" Derek asked.

"Somewhere without a jukebox," said Mike.

# Chapter Twenty-Two

Janney, Derek and Mike stood at the curb of the main road, waiting for a taxi to come by. They all felt the cold air and there was still a chance for more rain.

Mike had drunk wine on top of his pizza, as well as the two beers waiting for Finlay, then the whisky Finlay offered, all more than he wanted. He was telling himself, '*Stupid. Stupid.*' The extra oxygen was having its usual effect.

Mike now knew pizza and whisky did not mix well. Mixing it all with other drinks had not helped; neither was walking around. He needed to sit down. Leaning forward over the curb might now be a very bad idea. His car was a walking distance, but he knew he was unable to drive.

Derek was watching Janney and Mike. He could see Mike was ill. He looked at the boxes. He was going to stay with the two of them—there were stories to hear.

"Mike!" said Janney as a thought struck. "Would that cafe we sat in be open now?"

Mike brightened, "Good idea. Might be open just about now. I could really do with something other than alcohol." '*A sink or toilet might also be a good idea,*' he hoped.

Eventually a taxi came. Once they squeezed in, it occurred to Mike they were going out of Derek's way.

Mike began to quickly apologise. "Don't worry," said Derek. "There are plenty of taxis." He told Mike to calm down and take it easy.

They arrived at the market cafe, which opened its doors at 10 pm. The tables were empty, except for two old men in the corner, drinking tea, getting away from the cold and finding company. They were waiting for the early market workers and the first of the morning newspapers would be dropped off later inside the market forecourt.

The elderly woman behind the counter greeted Mike again as an old friend, as did the two men drinking tea. Janney still wondered how Mike got to know all these people.

Mike sat down and tried to settle his stomach. He called out, "Janney! Could you get me a coffee, please, milk, no sugar?"

Derek went to the counter with Janney. He could not bring himself to shout an order towards Janney. Janney was taking it all in her stride. She asked Derek what he wanted; Derek left her to sit with Mike.

*'Seems as if Janney has found a new friend,'* thought Derek, *'but who on earth is this guy?'*

"Did you get all you wanted?" Derek said, looking at the boxes.

"What I want now is something for a headache, settle my stomach," said Mike.

Janney brought three mugs of coffee to the table and waited till everyone was ready. She turned to Mike, "Now! What's with the tapes?"

Mike relaxed and sank back into the plastic chair.

"It occurred to me that these are rehearsal tapes. The music stops and starts, sometimes the tape is still running, people talk, argue, gossip, for hours on end. They date back several months or so. Brian could be on a lot of them. He may have said something worth hearing. We had to get these before the police got the same idea and took them away."

Derek seemed confused "What's wrong with the police listening?"

Mike turned to Derek, "They would not spot the same things we might. Once the police got their hands on these, they would never let us near them. We can give them to the police once we are finished."

Derek thought back, "Yesterday when I was hiding in my flat, I remembered Brian telling me months ago he had been burgled. I didn't tell that to the police at the party."

"What was stolen?" Mike's discomfort completely disappeared.

"Brian told me he had two tapes at his flat. They were taken, as well as all his music manuscripts, all his arrangements. I asked him if his flutes were stolen, he had three and they were worth money. He said 'No,' nothing else was touched. Later, I gained the impression that Brian had an idea of who did it—not immediately though. He was a bit clueless like that; he never wanted to examine people's motives. People were a bit of a mystery to Brian."

"Anyway, it was weeks later he suddenly started asking to speak to Malcolm. I felt sure that's why he asked for an invite to the party. Who knows! It might have been related back to the burglary. He didn't speak much about it, but I once heard him mutter, "It was all unfair"."

Mike turned to Janney; he began to look very ill. He told her it might all be a waste of time, but would she take the tapes and listen to them? He explained again how maybe they could contain relevant information. It might take her a day or more, but it was all they had to work with.

Janney saw it had to be her. She was the only one who might understand the conversations, the banter. It was not a hard decision: she could visit one of the studios, bring the tapes, set up a machine. She turned towards Derek, she told him she was taking that day off to do it, she stressed he had to keep quiet to everyone, only tell Malcolm.

Mike suddenly looked at the toilet door, said a quick 'pardon,' put his hand on his mouth, got up and disappeared into the toilet. After a few minutes, he returned, "A lot better now."

Mable, the lady behind the counter, came to the table. "Are you alright, Love?"

"I am fine Mabel, thanks," said Mike. "I just wrote a poem about cheese."

"We will have to try pepperoni next time," said Janney.

Mike smiled, "Without beer or whisky." Janney smiled back. She felt the café becoming a friendly place.

The three sat and talked about the celebrities who were bound to talk to the press. The newspapers would eventually track down the three guests affected by the punch. The coroner was giving a verdict in a few days. If anything, new could be found, it had better be found quickly.

# Chapter Twenty-Three

Derek hardly slept but decided that morning he would go to work. He thought someone might be watching for him as he left his apartment. He caught the bus, but no one bothered him.

He entered the building where he worked the last few years and walked up the stairs. He passed the typing pool. He saw he had their attention.

Finding a girlfriend no longer carried any real interest. He remembered the waitress he met at the party. She had seemed nice, until poor Brian fell. Her name was Sue. Looking at Brian on the gravel, then looking at him kneeling there with tears in his eyes, she appeared embarrassed. She slowly backed away, then disappeared. A dead body in front of them, her first thought was not to get involved. He had not expected that.

Derek walked past his desk and towards Malcolm Offen's office. He had never entered without permission before but this time he entered without knocking and walked over to the chair in front of Malcolm's desk and sat down.

Malcolm said nothing except "Have a seat", while Derek was still adjusting himself in the chair.

Derek told Malcolm all the events of the night before. He even told of Mike's trip to the toilet.

"Janney said to let you know she would be spending the day at a studio, I am not sure which one, but it might be the one Brian worked most in."

"Thanks, Derek, how are you? In yourself?"

"Seems like a while ago now," said Derek.

Malcolm began talking but this time his points were said slowly and with a lot of consideration.

"You might find yourself treating others differently now, at least for a week or two. Watching someone die unexpectedly, especially a friend, affects different people in different ways, It's a personal thing, like grief. It becomes private knowledge. Watch yourself! An experience like that can bring lots to the surface. Stuff also gets buried and then can reappear later."

Malcolm took time to pause, he was a little unsure of the state Derek might be in.

"Derek, I have no wish to appear trivial, but it might be in the interest of others if you did not discuss anything said yesterday with anyone else, or about anything you might believe happened for that matter, except when you speak to the police of course. Shut up about the tapes, until the police ask a specific question. Talking about them would make Janney and Mike look bad. The tapes have not been shown as relevant yet. The police will get them soon enough. The police will no doubt call to speak to you. Brian came to the party on your invite. Have they been in touch?"

"No! I do not answer the door or telephone anymore."

"See how much work you can do today but take it easy, go home early if you feel like it. Do not let anyone bother you. If anyone upsets you, remember it's part of the fallout."

Malcolm continued to watch Derek carefully, he sensed feelings were still raw. "If you feel any amount of stress or aggravation while you're with others, distance yourself, walk away. Give yourself space whenever you want it, take time off if you want. I will telephone Inspector Hawkins and tell him to call you at your desk to arrange an interview."

Derek nodded absently. "Thanks. What about you, how are you?"

Malcolm gave a very friendly smile. "Derek, I do not know if you will go far in life, but people will always like you."

"You are the only person to ask me that since Saturday. I am fine. Thank you for asking."

Derek felt a little better. "I better get back to work." Malcolm watched him walk through the door.

Last week any conversation between the two would have been very different. Malcolm reflected on how people can change and how quickly. There are learning experiences, even if ultimately beneficial, some people might do better without. Then again, who might we have become without them?

*'A question with many different answers,'* thought Malcolm, *'a notion better considered by theatre critics than philosophers.'*

Derek returned to his desk and looked at his tray. He lifted all the memos, letters and phone messages from the day before. One thought seemed to resonate, that it was all so unimportant.

He had always enjoyed systems, organising information. Today it all seemed ridiculous. He could see it, and he knew it in his heart—it had always been ridiculous.

*'Is this what I wanted to do with my whole life?'* He felt he had been so stupid.

He gave himself a few moments, then he saw his job for what it truly was, a means to an end. He knew he had to see a bigger picture, but that had never happened for him. Instinctively he knew that the big picture, whatever it was, was something you didn't look to find—too big for that.

*'I can't do this anymore; how can anyone do this*?' He thought.

He imagined again finding a partner, someone else to be part of his life, a girlfriend. Maybe that might bring a sort of purpose. The right girl could bring value to time spent. He realised he still had no idea what sort of partner he wanted, whatever it was she would offer, or what she might even want from him.

Derek laughed to himself. He saw that it was always going to be down to chance, but he would stand a better chance, maybe even become a happier man, if he didn't waste his time always trying to be the nice guy, just so others would prefer his company—truthfully, just tolerate his company.

Even that answer smacked of a compromise or a surrender to something he couldn't identify. Derek felt as if his brain was a cake that was slowly collapsing in the oven.

He could not lose the image of Brian lying in front of him, broken, then covered over by a sheet, gone forever. He had been the one to bring Brian to the party. Brian smiled when he told him, he was grateful; he thanked him.

It was suddenly important to be someplace else. He wondered if he kept moving, maybe he could find himself someplace else, somewhere with better people.

# Chapter Twenty-Four

Janney turned up at the ZZZ Studio at 11.30am. She had needed a late lie in. In the early hours, she had dropped Mike off in a taxi at his address, then got Derek home, before giving the taxi driver her own address.

She had started the evening with enough money to pay her way but had not put her hand in her pocket once. Just as well, it left her enough to pay everyone's taxi fares.

She travelled by taxi again that morning to ZZZ Studios, or Triple Z or Z3 Studios as it became referred to. The taxi was necessary because of the two long stacks of tape boxes bound by ribbon she carried into the studio's reception area.

She gave her name at the reception desk and asked for the general manager, Phillip Bennett. Janney had met Phillip Bennett once. She was unsure if she would be remembered.

The receptionist smiled, "Mr Bennett is not available. May I ask the nature of your business?"

Janney felt a little torn. She knew the girl was just doing her job, but could not help thinking,

*'If I told you all about my business, would you then change your mind about him being available?'* She pulled herself back from such stupid reasoning.

It was a strange thing—she recalled times like these when her confidence completely left her, as if it had never really existed. She would need to take a moment to look for it, remember it, rediscover it.

This situation brought other memories back again, from years past. She used to tell herself, '*Confidence is just a word to refer to.*' Right now, she needed a bit more than just confidence; she needed to draw back on something from her history, to push through an imaginary obstacle.

The events of Saturday night, the evening she spent with Mike; thinking about those moments made her feel as if all her anxieties were stepping aside, if only for just for a little while.

When she opened her mouth, housing estate accent and all, it was not with the pretence of a confident girl talking. It was going to be Janney Malone talking.

But first, '*Always necessary to first size up the person you're speaking with, never patronise,*' she thought.

Janney started to feel better. '*It is what it is, I am what I am*,' she thought. '*No need to try and imagine a whole set of attitudes as part of whoever I want to be. You become less real when you depend on things which are not real.*'

Janney finally saw she had a job to do and there was really no need to be put off by anyone trying to slow her down. No need to be stupid about this, that can come back and bite you.

She stood full square in front of the reception desk.

Janney spoke very calmly, "My name is Janney Malone. I have no appointment. I am not expected! I have come from the MCM head office. Mr Bennett knows me. I feel sure will see me. Could you please tell him I am here?"

The receptionist continued to smile. She liked being unimpressed. "Mr Bennett is in a meeting. He may be unavailable for some time. Please take a seat. I will contact him once he is available."

Janney gave an even broader smile. "Thank you for all of that. It was good to know. Please tell him once he is available. Please also tell him where I am. In the meantime, I require the use of a studio, immediate use! Thank you! Please call someone in charge of studio time. Please ask if they would come down to speak with me."

At this point, the receptionist's face lost all expression.

"Please take a seat. I will have someone come and speak with you."

Janney sat down and waited. After about 15 minutes, she tried to think of something nice to say to the receptionist, maybe introduce a bit of sisterhood. It might offset the abruptness. Might even get her a cup of tea.

Eventually, Janney saw a man standing in front of her.

Long-haired, very tall and thin, with a Ban the Bomb T-shirt. There was no way a girl with her background was going to be intimidated by this guy.

"Hello! I have come from the MCM head office. I am sorry but I am in a bit of a hurry. I mentioned it to your receptionist," she looked to her side. "Sorry! I did not catch your name. I mentioned that I need a studio. That's not strictly true. I only need a room with a reel-to-reel tape machine. I have the tapes," she gestured at the boxes.

Janney felt more and more in her stride. "I may also need headphones. I will need someone to set up the machine to play the tapes. I also wish to speak with Phillip Bennett when he is free."

The long-haired T-shirt gave the distinct impression that he had not expected he would need to explain himself or have any sort of conversation.

He spoke slowly, "I am afraid we do not have a studio or a machine available."

Janney continued to smile and spoke slowly. '*Remember, No Patronising*!' "Please find an empty room. Please place a tape machine in the room. Have someone available to set the machine up to play the tapes. If that is not possible, please contact Malcolm Offen at MCM head office and tell him Janney Malone is here and wishes to speak with him. I can give you the number if you need it."

"You're Janney Malone?" The long-haired T-shirt leaned forward. It sounded more of a question than a statement.

"Yes! Didn't the receptionist," she looked again at the desk, "Sorry! I still don't have your name. Didn't she tell you?

"You were there on Saturday when Brian died?" The long-haired T-shirt was now taking a step back, stunned. At this statement, the receptionist was out from behind her desk.

"Please follow me into another waiting area. My name is Anna, by the way." Janney followed. The long-haired T-shirt carried the boxes.

'*Must remember to use all the vowel sounds,*' thought Janney. She continued to explain she only needed to listen to some tapes, she would be quiet, no bother. She said she would have gone elsewhere if that had been possible. Janney learnt long ago it's best to be humble when you're getting all you want.

Within an hour, she sat in front of a machine, with headphones on the table. She picked up a box with the earliest date; the date still not crossed over. She had asked for it to be placed onto the reels. She picked up the headphones and began to listen.

About 30 minutes later, the door opened, and Phillip Bennett entered.

"Hello, Janney, good to see you again."

"Hello, Phillip, I am afraid I made a bit of a nuisance of myself."

"So, I hear, it seems you have been throwing your weight about."

"I must apologise about that, Phillip! Since Saturday, a few of us have been running around trying to find out what happened to Brian Nicholls. In the early hours, this very morning in fact, I was given these tapes. They may have Brian's voice on them. They might be important."

Janney stopped and waited for Phillip to speak. There was no actual reason for Janney to stop speaking but Janney had seen people behave and knew that if you believe you're in charge, you do not have to do all the talking.

She knew she was not in charge but there was no reason to show she was aware of that. Politeness carried several purposes.

Phillip continued to be silent.

Janney gave it a few more seconds and again broke the silence, "I know I could have telephoned but I was not sure if I would be given the runaround." There was more silence.

"I decided I would come in first and try to speak with you, but you were busy, so I took a few chances with your staff. I don't really have a lot of weight."

Phillip gave a short smile. "Might have been handled better. My staff have their own job to do, you know. What makes you think Brian is on the tapes?"

Janney told Phillip the whole story. Phillip asked no questions. Finally, he said, "Will you be alright now? Do you need lunch or anything? Have you been introduced to John?"

"Is that the guy in the T-shirt?"

Phillip smiled, "Yes, he and Brian were friends. They worked together. He wants to help. You can ask for him. He will do anything you want."

"Thanks! Phillip, this might all come to nothing, but it's all we have."

Phillip became silent again. Janney watched Phillip and thought to herself, '*This is someone who takes his time. He really knows how to make the silence trick work.*'

Phillip finally spoke, "I have heard rumours of what happened. I hope they are all untrue. Good luck."

"Can I speak with you again before I leave? I might need to come back again tomorrow."

"If I am still here. I will let Anna know at the front desk," Phillip stood up to leave.

"You know, while I was being very arrogant, Anna never lost her cool and was very helpful. Please tell her I appreciate it and that I apologise for when I appeared rude."

Phillip smiled again, "I think that is for you to say. Phillip left and closed the door.

'*One for the sisterhood,*' thought Janney. She resisted the urge to punch the air.

# Chapter Twenty-Five

Janney pressed the button on the machine and saw the tape slowly turn. She glanced down at the other twenty-odd boxes. It was going to be a long haul.

She had taken the tape with the earliest date and was going to try to listen to all of them in chronological order. After an hour, she learnt more about one aspiring band, their girlfriends and why they hated their manager than she ever wanted to know.

She called out for John. She needed a break. Maybe John knew something useful about Brian; maybe John wanted to know more.

John came immediately. Janney asked for a coffee and if John was free. it might be nice to talk. John came back with two coffees. He was happy to talk.

"How long did you know Brian? Janney asked.

"Since I came here, nearly two years. Brian was a real asset. He would help anyone with anything, didn't need to be asked."

"Did you work together?"

"Sort of. I am not a musician. I am a bit of a sound engineer. More of a dogsbody really."

"Is that why they sent you to deal with me?"

"Maybe! You might not remember, but we have spoken on the telephone a couple of times."

"Sorry."

"Well, it was a while ago. You have a lot of tapes to get through. About '40 hours' worth."

Janney's face showed that she hated this idea.

"Let me show you how to replace the tape. If you're looking for something specific, it might be possible to speed things along."

"Oh! Do tell."

John pointed to the counter on the machine, "If you press fast forward, a hundred units on the counter is about 10 minutes, then listen. If it's just music and you're not interested, then repeat until you hear a passage you want. You could get through half of these in a few hours."

Janney felt a bit stupid. It had only required a bit of thought.

Janney could hear her mother again, talking calmly after listening to Janney screaming the odds at her as a teenager, '*You waste so much time ordering people about, you can miss what you can do for yourself.*'

"What did you see on Saturday?" John asked.

Janney told as much as she could. John listened intently. He already knew much of what he was told, but he wanted to hear it again from someone who was there. If he heard it firsthand, he felt a little closer to his friend.

John started to leave. Janney asked him to come back before he left for the day. He said he would; he thanked her for the talk.

Janney started to get through the tapes. After about two hours, she had finished most of the early tapes.

Janney could often tell where some bands had only one accomplished musician. She thought it might be a good idea to get good musicians from different bands and introduce them. She would have to bring up the idea with Malcolm.

She continued with the tapes and then suddenly, instead of guitars and drums, she heard flute music. Janney knew the tune being played. She listened for five minutes and then she heard Brian's voice. She quickly pressed rewind and caught the point where another band's recording finished, revealing the partial earlier recording of flute music which remained at the end of the tape.

Janney looked at the dates on the box label; at all the dates struck off. She realised the more recent recording had run over much of the flute music.

She searched through the dates on the labels, there were no close dates to that specific recording. It was clear that there were a few weeks where no recordings were made. Some tapes might be missing.

Her heart was pounding. Janney did not want to feel alone with this information. Janney called John back into the room.

"John! If you've got a mo. I need some thoughts on this."

The tape was rewound again. The flute music began. The tune was being played backwards and forwards. It changed in tone and detail as it was played again and again. It was clear the player was improvising or trying to compose.

Janney and John both glanced at each other as they listened. They both knew the tune. Brian's voice cut in.

"What do you think?" Brian said. The response was unclear.

The flute music continued and then Brian spoke again, "I could blend this in with a similar piece on piano."

"Try it," said another voice. The tape finished. Both knew that other voice—it was Johnny Lately.

John stared into space. He said what Janney already knew, "That flute music was on 'Slipped away,' the record Lately released a few weeks ago."

John stared at the floor. Both made no sound for ten or twenty seconds. "Tommy Vinton produced that record. I am getting him down here." John raced out the door.

Janney tried to slow her emotions. It was clear this might be why Brian wanted to speak to Malcolm. '*It must be*,' thought Janney.

She realised she had to speak to Malcolm. She went out to the reception, but Anna was getting ready to go home. Janney explained anxiously that she had to speak to Malcolm Offen. Anna saw something important had happened.

Janney gave Anna the number and asked her to fetch her if she got Malcolm on the line. Anna agreed to do it and Janney went back to the tape machine. John and Tommy Vinton were waiting.

"Mr Vinton, could you please listen to this recording?

The tape played. Tommy Vinton kept looking at his fingernails.

"I do not like talking about people behind their backs or making accusations without proof." Tommy Vinton looked as if he were ready to leave.

Janney tried to push away from an interrogation and into a conversation. "Did that sound like Brian was composing to you? Was that the background melody on 'Slipped Away'?

"Could be, maybe."

"What do you remember from the recording session of 'Slipped Away'?"

Tommy Vinton collected his thoughts. It was clear these people were going to take him at his word, might even act on his word.

Tommy Vinton had a lifelong aversion to getting involved in other people's business. He could never stand the idea of people relying on some vague statement he might make, then acting on it, or maybe being misquoted on some quick answer he gave to an important question.

"Johnny Lately played me 'Slipped Away' on his guitar. I was asked to make a record with the man. Before a date was set, he contacted me and said he had some written arrangements for the song he wanted to add. He gave me written arrangements for flute and piano. He asked if I would bring in two more musicians to the sessions, flute and piano, which I did. It all became a bit of a success."

"Did you get the impression he had written the arrangements?"

Tommy Vinton was being asked for an opinion, an opinion he had carried for a while. He finally let loose some of the anger he felt since recording the record.

He said adamantly, "Johnny Lately knew nothing, not a single thing, about making or writing a music arrangement."

"If the musicians asked a simple question about the sheets, the music, he just ignored them and referred the matter to me. He kept his mouth shut the whole time, except when he was trying to sing. The music sheets were complex. There were key changes between the flute and piano pieces that were unusual, like nothing I had heard before."

Tommy Vinton gave a long breath, "When it was over, he grabbed the sheets away. I even congratulated him! He said he had other songs he wanted to put on an album. He wanted them all in a similar vein." Tommy Vinton then finally relaxed. He looked like a man who had got something off his chest.

Janney thanked him. She could hardly contain herself. She walked over and gave John a hug. She buried her head into his belly. She went out to Anna who told her Malcolm Offen was waiting for her call.

Malcolm answered on the first ring. Janney spent the next half hour explaining everything that had been said. Malcolm said very little. He thanked her and told her to wait in reception until he called again. Anna listened to the whole conversation. She looked trapped inside her chair.

After more than an hour, the telephone rang again. Anna gave the handset to Janney. Anna was so glad she stayed, so glad the phone was fixed onto the desk.

Malcolm said the police were on their way. They wanted the tapes. They very much wanted to speak with her. Once she was finished, he would be at David's house. He asked if she would please come over for a little chat. If she felt ready.

Janney sat and waited for the police to come. It could not have come sooner—Anna would not shut up. The woman had become obsessed with Saturday. She then started asking questions on how to apply for Janney's job. Janney thought hard about Malcolm's instructions saying, '*No comment.*'

If her mother ever heard Janney say '*No comment*' to a receptionist, or to anybody for that matter, Janney would have been silenced with a look. The Irish never try to speak like the English.

# Chapter Twenty-Six

Malcolm sat back in his chair and smiled. He had a few things to consider. *'Let's see if I can still let the old mind reach out to the infinite,'* he laughed as he considered himself. His first instructions on how to meditate came from speaking to a Buddhist priest. In New York of all places.

It had taken him years of trying to absorb life in America before he seriously considered learning meditation. "It's better than sitting around doing nothing, I suppose." An old joke he carried with him, allow him to be witty in bars.

One day he was staring down at the brown liquid he was about to drink; his eyes fell into the lights within the glass. He listened again, just for a moment, an instant, to all he had heard that day, ideas, impressions, fears, all the views he never asked for, but were taught as necessary for a good life.

He had a distrust of most organised religions; however, he still took on board the basic theories of newly accepted spiritual thoughts. It was part of being connected to the emerging Beatnik generation, a good idea if you wanted to keep up with social conventions. *'Poets and cool jazz musicians.'* Peer groups came in many different forms within the music business.

Looking into the glass an idea revealed itself to him: strip away all thought, all the minutiae that occupy every minute of each day, prevent yourself from lurching forward to the next thought. Instead exist within a single moment and let the void take over, see what thoughts visit you without invitation.

Meditation practices were varied; many were not for him. One day something happened as he sat still for an hour on a yoga mat in Upper New York. His eyes had been closed, the room quiet, his mind began to see shapes moving and this became enough.

If he followed the shapes, constructing and breaking them down, he could see patterns within his memories. He could recognise the bad ideas, bad thought directions, all the things he could turn away from, see from a distance, he saw a way he could slowly form better decisions, better for him.

After some instruction, he learnt how to study his breathing. After some more instruction, he eventually learnt how to focus and relax into his thoughts.

A year later he saw he had to return to the UK.

He grew a deep desire to escape American society, the politics and the distaste for foreign or new ideas. He came to examine himself, at his core, he still had to reconcile himself with the man he was before the war, the man he became in the war, the man he was now, the man he presented each day to others.

During his time in the States, the self-righteousness handed out in everyday conversation begun to get under his skin. The paranoia, coupled with isolationist views, all of it intruded into the ideas he carried around of his reasonable self, he wondered what he was turning into.

Malcolm straightened his fingers and slowly opened his eyes. He could recall Johnny Lately. Meditation had improved his capacity for memory.

He remembered watching him backstage on a tour. Johnny Lately could not tolerate anyone else being popular or even good company. It was not enough for Johnny Lately to succeed; he could not share credit for anything.

Malcolm pulled himself out from his 'quiet time.' He knew whenever he allowed his mind to rest and soar, he should not allow ugly thoughts to make clouds.

He picked up the telephone and called David. After repeating to his cousin all the news of Janney's call, he could hear David unable to stand still.

He heard Mike beside the phone, he was trying to calm David down. '*Good, Good,*' thought Malcolm. He asked David to hand the telephone to Mike.

'*Mike is a good man,*' thought Malcolm. He had to smile. He caught on immediately that Mike, for all his esoteric references to Zen philosophy, was just trying not to reveal much. He was confident Mike would find his own level, his own journey, when ready and when capable of facing himself.

Malcolm spoke to Mike and then again to David and it was agreed they would wait for Janney to get in touch, maybe they would get a call from Inspector Hawkins. They should decide, but only after a discussion, what information should be released to the public. Important to keep in mind Johnny Lately was still roaming around.

Janney travelled by police car to the station. '*Mum would not be proud,*' she thought. At least they had not called for her at her mother's address.

"Never ever have the police come knocking at my door," she used to tell Janney, pointing her hard finger, as Janney sat quite as a 12-year-old eating cornflakes.

Janney saw the tapes taken away and found herself sitting opposite Inspector Hawkins.

"Thank you for coming, Ms Malone."

Janney sat under a moving hanging light bulb, looking at the edges of the shadows, moving back and forth, on the table. *'Who said the police have no manners?'* she thought.

She then realised she had never heard anyone say that. It was the sort of thing you always assumed.

"Could you please give me the same information you gave to Mr Malcolm Offen, step by step please, right from the beginning?"

Janney went through the whole story, from the very start, from walking into the Back Door, with lots of extra little details. Inspector Hawkins hardly said a word. He took the odd note. *'Just notes for later.'* Janney kept wondering which of the things she said were important,

She told the inspector what little background information she knew of Johnny Lately. She emphasised she never saw him, or Brian Nicholls arrive at the party. She never saw Johnny Lately leave.

Inspector Hawkins put his notepad down. "Thank you, Miss Malone. Now, do you have any thoughts you want to share about what you saw Saturday evening?"

"What do you mean?"

"Well, you might have seen something that seemed curious to you, something that was said, or which occurred that you thought was strange. People often keep ideas like that to themselves."

Janney didn't see what he was getting at, "The place was full of ego-driven celebrities, who were not allowed to leave. There was a lot of strange behaviour going on."

"Let's explore that thought for a moment. What did you see happen immediately following Mr Nicholls' fall?

"Some people were curious, some people argued, and there appeared to be a rush to get to the cars. Some people had already left. People kept raising their voices, asking where their drivers were, some woman would not shut up about her coat. She kept on saying it was stolen."

"Oh yes!" said Inspector Hawkins, "I remember her, she was still there long after you left, would not shut up. We found her coat in the end, someone in a side room had been asleep on top of it, using it as a cushion, fur is good for that."

Janney took another moment to recall those moments, "Some parked cars were getting in the way of others in the rush. People had walked down the path to the front gate to get away as soon as they could."

"Excuse me, who walked to the gate?"

"I do not know. It was dark. I only saw the backs of people, several of them. Not everyone had arrived by driving through the gate. Some had cars parked in the streets outside and arrived by walking through the gate. I don't think any of the cars parked inside had a chance to leave before the police arrived."

Inspector Hawkings continued to watch Janney in silence.

Then Janney spoke again. She wondered if somehow, she was being judged. "If Lately was in the house at the time of Brian's death, he might have left immediately. The police would not have seen him. They had not arrived yet."

Janney felt she had to speak up for David "David Offen asked the staff to request that everyone remain. He said you would want to speak with everyone."

The inspector said, "He walked in and walked out, he had no car!"

"Some didn't, some of the women didn't either."

"You would have only seen his back."

Janney could see the inspector concentrating; then she saw a thought cross his face. He lifted his hand to his eyes as if he could hardly believe what had just occurred. He got up quickly, excused himself and left Janney alone for 30 minutes, then returned.

"Miss Malone, you have provided exceptional assistance. Thank you! Once I have made some further enquiries, I may ask you to return to give a statement."

"Of course, I have clearly said something—what was it?"

"It may come to nothing, but after I have made enquiries, we might all be the wiser. Do you need a lift home?"

"No, thank you, I have places to go, people to see." Janney had already decided, before she went onto David Offen's house, she would first go and give Finlay Bruce a heads-up.

In truth, Janney also never wanted to sit in another police car. When she thought of it, she did not want anyone to ever see her get into or out of a police car, ever! Some Irish memories really did run deep.

# Chapter Twenty-Seven

Malcolm sat in David's house. He asked that Mike stay and wait for Janney. Malcolm knew David would want to analyse the latest information to death. The other truth was that David did not have many friends he could trust with personal information—fewer than he imagined he had; that was becoming clear.

The three sat in the kitchen. It had been amusing to Malcolm to watch Mike bait David with cryptic comments that David, in turn, would only pretend to understand.

In the middle of a conversation, Mike would drop a Zen comment that was clearly irrelevant or deliberately convoluted; David would still nod his head in agreement. Malcolm sat stony-faced for fear of laughing out loud.

Janney telephoned David again and was immediately invited over. She told David that she was enroute to the Back Door to first speak with Finlay Bruce. David said they would wait for her; he insisted she use a taxi.

David had received a few telephone calls that day. Some people left messages through third parties and had cancelled meetings that had been set up for the following week. Some people he knew for years were refusing to take his calls.

David expected managers were now speaking with their clients, taking on extra duties, finding new deals, new promoters. The managers would want to appear useful, let their clients witness them taking bold action. At the same time, pocketing additional management fees for all the new duties. David had seen it before. He had done the same thing himself; it had always been a good money spinner.

The newspapers were in touch again. There were many requests for interviews but always politely refused. The telephone callers began to give oblique references to LSD. It was clear the papers had only part of the story and were fishing for a comment they could then quote.

One paper asked for an exclusive interview and promised that if it were granted, the coverage given would be favourable. The threat was clear. David found some sort of ancestral family attitude swell inside him, but he put the telephone down. For a second, he was ready to lose everything if he could just burn down and bury the paper at the same time.

The three men drank coffee and realised they had no strategy but to wait. Earlier that day, David had tried to contact the family of the girls at the party affected by the LSD. He was told they had been advised to have no communication with him. No more needed to be said. People were lawyering up.

Janney approached the Back Door and saw Finlay Bruce outside supervising the crowd. He had booked the band for that night a few months previously. In the interim, the band released a record which was now high in the charts. If he had tried to book the same band the day before, he would not been able to afford them.

The band had been so grateful for the gig at the time of booking they decided to still honour the original agreement, as well as at the original fee.

The crowd was much larger than usual. Finlay was giving instructions that no one was allowed in wearing football colours, following the local semi-final match played earlier in the day.

Finlay spotted Janney and walked over. He told her Mike had delivered the new tapes that morning.

It was clear he was in an effervescent mood. He explained how this band wanted it known to everyone, discreetly, of course, they were honouring some sort of working-class word of honour ethic by keeping to their early booking. Then Finlay laughed.

"Working class hell! These are all ex-Cambridge students." He laughed again, "No way would anyone working class charge less than their full rate."

"Good luck to them," said Janney.

"Yeah, you're right," said Finlay. "Good luck to them."

Janney told Finlay she was coming by to bring him up to date. She had not planned to say much, but she saw now she could get away letting him think she had intended to. She saw he was too preoccupied to speak. Finlay thanked her but asked if she could come by tomorrow.

Finlay then spoke over his shoulder, "I am out in the morning but will be back by 2pm." Janney said she would see him tomorrow and left him as he started running around like a chicken on the pavement, completely absorbed with his biggest-ever midweek crowd.

When Janney reached David's house, she found them all watching the news on the television.

In the last few days, a few big political events occupied the television media. As far as the newspapers were concerned, they continued to offer speculation on Brian's death, with repeated references to David's reputation.

The four retired to the kitchen table, eager to hear what Janney had to say. She spoke of the tapes, Brian's voice, everything Tommy Vinton had said, the interview at the police station. Without much else said, it became clear it was best to wait until the police got hold of Mr Johnny Lately.

David became increasingly annoying. He kept returning to Janney's conversation with Inspector Hawkins.

He spoke as if he thought it was possible to still drag some new morsel of information from Janney on what the inspector could have imagined so interesting.

Mike remained quiet at the table except to tell Janney how well she had done. Malcolm had said the same but then he snapped at David.

"For goodness' sake, man, you have heard everything she has said. You can't always invent something new out of what's already been said. Even if you did, we cannot act on it."

Malcolm quickly adjusted his tone. He put his hand on David's shoulder and spoke calmly, "Don't worry. Man, one way or another, the field will change in the next few days. In the meantime, everyone keeps their mouths shut, or we might wind up knee-high in defamation suits."

Mike spoke up, "Ring around, make sure no payments are made to him from the company. That might bring him out of his hole."

Malcolm made a fist and gave the table a small bump.

"Right! Right! I will give Bill Hawkins a ring tomorrow. Mike, you and Janney really deserve a lot of thanks. Well done."

David felt a little more comfortable. He could hear positive voices in the room. "Yeah, thanks a lot to you both. You all have been good friends."

Mike could see the mood shift; he told David, "Resistance to the unforeseen is the root of suffering."

David took a breath, paused, gave a thought and then said, "Mike! Look, as it happens, I might even agree with that one. Let's not just disappear down a rabbit hole. OK! Stop saying that stuff. We are all getting along here."

Mike could not resist another one, "A muddy pool clears itself."

David studied Mike. He still felt tense from Malcolms outburst, he also felt as if he was being prodded with a stick. He had asked nicely for Mike to stop. He had finally had enough; this had gone on long enough and David felt sick of it. It was time now to put the guy in his place.

"Mike, I feel I should make a point here. I make a lot more money than you. I know somewhere on this planet that doesn't really matter, but it's still important somewhere else. In fact, I think I will pay you out of petty cash."

David then gave a look towards Mike as if to say, "Go on, answer that."

Mike adjusted his seat for that statement. He thought for a few seconds. "Thank you for putting that out there. Dave. It needed to be said. Or maybe you just needed to say it, for yourself anyway. Don't give up on your dreams, Dave."
David felt he had him, "I just felt relaxed enough in your company to say it, Mike, I know you're good for that."

Mike had to hand it back. "Well, I know you are practised in spending money, Dave, but have you ever tried to be aware of what it should be spent on?"

"That's a work in progress, Mike. Should I ask for your advice on it? All you seem to be good for is advice."

Malcolm saw things were about to turn very nasty. He stepped in quickly before more was said, "I am sure Dave will accept guidance from us all on that subject one day."

Malcolm bore his energy down hard on the two of them. David and Mike just turned and sat back with their drinks and looked away from each other. It was clear the tension of the whole day had taken a toll.

Janney watched the two of them and started to wonder if she even really needed to go to university. These two needed lessons she learnt from her mother a long time ago.

Middle-class people and polite arguments always appeared ridiculous to Janney. If they wanted to know how to do it properly, they should try listening to a shouting match in an Irish pub. At least there they could pick up a few original quotes. She looked for a way to break the bad mood that had crept into the room, spoiling the earlier optimism.

Janney turned to the group. "I am going to see Finlay Bruce again tomorrow morning. Bring him up to date, on the tapes at least. He might still know more if I tell him about the tapes. It all happened in his basement, after all."

Malcolm slapped his hands together and blew apart the cloud in the room, "We have a plan."

"I will call Bill Hawkins tomorrow. Now who is for getting some beer and fish and chips in and watching the football on the box? Two semi-final matches today, no one say what the scores are if they already know them."

# Chapter Twenty-Eight

The next morning, Janney walked from her flat towards the market area. She had got home late after watching the football with the three men. '*Another thing to strike off my 'to do list' as well as put on my 'never need to do again list'* she felt she needed to walk alone.

She approached the window of the market cafe. It appeared completely full. The same woman was behind the counter. Janney wondered how many hours she put in, or if she maybe owned the cafe.

She didn't know if she could ever do a job like that. '*If I had to, I suppose I could. If I absolutely had to, I would,*' she thought again. '*I suppose that applies to everybody.*'

The sky had finally turned bright. Janney bought a couple of papers and decided to walk to the Back Door and read them there. She needed sunlight on her arms.

Once she arrived and walked through the door, she realised and only for the first time, what a large venue the Back Door was. She had never been there in the daytime, had never seen it so empty.

She saw a few people cleaning and only one person drinking at the bar.

She spotted Tom, one of the managers. Finlay had introduced them. He helped when the tapes had been carried out two nights before.

"Hi Tom, is there anyone in the studio?"

"No, it's been empty all night."

"Finlay said I could go down and have a listen to two of the tapes. Do you mind if I go downstairs?" Janney didn't care that it was a lie. *'What the hell?'*

"Sure. Are you going to hang around?"

"Yeah! I'm waiting for Finlay."

"Well, go ahead, it's empty. I think the door is unlocked."

She walked to the staircase, went downstairs and entered the studio. She saw the new boxes of tapes, stacked in the corner. None had been opened. *'I bet that band last night couldn't get away fast enough. Wouldn't have blamed them.'*

She saw the two old tape boxes she and Mike had left behind. She knew by now how to fix them up to play.

She would just listen, while she waited and see if they were worth anything. She fitted the first tape into the reel-to-reel. Once the music began, she sat down and started to read the papers. No need for headphones.

The music was immediately forgettable. Two or three guitar players and a drummer ran through the hits of the day, with nothing to recommend any of them. To Janney they seemed to be just going through the motions.

Janney heard the door close and looked up from the papers. Standing in front of her was Mr Johnny Lately.

"Hello, Janney. How have you been?"

Janney could not think of what to do next. "Fine, how are you?"

"Oh! Not so bad, do you mind if I turn this off?" He walked to the machine and flipped a switch. The room was silent again. Janney looked at the closed door. She knew no one would hear anything if she shouted.

Janney stood up, "Let's have a drink upstairs. We can talk." Janney rose from her chair.

"No! Let's talk here." Johnny Lately grabbed Janney's arm and sat her back in the chair. He moved a small table into her waist and then pushed her backwards, back, tight up against the wall. He put a small torn paper cup on the table.

"Don't let me see that cup move, not even a little bit."

"You can't treat me like this."

"Why can't I?"

"I will tell the police." Even as she said it, she knew she was wasting her time. Lately was walking around the room as if in a half-awake dream.

"He said, she said," he muttered. He turned to look at Janney. She could see he had not been sleeping, maybe existing on pills since Saturday. His eyes were like pinpricks.

"We are going to have a chat. I want to know what you have been doing." He started to raise his voice, "I want to know why everyone has been trying to interfere with my life."

Mike visited Malcolm at his office that morning. Malcolm had asked for some quick advice; the sort of quick advice lawyers would never just give.

MCM Plc had been dealing with some new private booking agents. Malcolm had received complaints.

The agents had been slyly encouraging venues and others to infer they were owned by or were acting as part of MCM Plc. They were trading on the company's reputation.

Mike made the point simply, "Any agreement your company makes with subcontractors should make clear they are under an active duty to leave no doubt, when dealing with others, that they are in fact independent and not agents acting for MCM Plc. Also make the point, just in casual conversation, no need to make threats. they all know what you are. You're a big company with a big legal department and you will drown anyone who messes with you, in both the final legal expenses and with bad press. It will not trouble you at all to lose a little money if it will dissuade others from taking liberties. The word will soon get around."

Mike was telling Malcolm what he already knew. Malcolm just wanted someone to say it out loud. Some companies were trying to get new business on MCM Plc coattails.

It had not been a legal consultation, no mention of payment, Malcolm had promised Mike lunch. As they were getting ready to leave, Malcolm put in a call to Inspector Hawkins.

"Hello, Bill. When are we going to catch up again? Why not come over to the house for drinks?"

"That sounds good, Malcolm. Do you have any idea where I can find Mr Johnny Lately?"

"No! Not a clue, why?"

"Malcolm, stay away from Johnny Lately. I intend to arrest him. Let me know immediately if you hear where he might be. Tell Miss Malone to stay away from him also. He is a very dangerous man."

# Chapter Twenty-Nine

Johnny Lately picked up a chair and sat opposite Janney. She could see he was unshaven and had a lot of dried sweat on his face. His whole body seemed quiet and relaxed. Whatever game he was playing, he was not acting. With a very calm voice, he began to speak.

"People are looking for me. Why is that?

"The police want to speak to everyone that was at the party. There are only a few people left to interview. You left before the police arrived."

"That's right, I left early. Saw you though, saw poor Brian flying, saw him land, that's when I left. Nothing at all to do with me, any of it. The party was over. I just walked out and left."

"Why don't you tell the police that?"

Lately smiled. "Maybe I will." He began to look around.

"I used to spend a lot of time down here with Brian. He was a nice guy, stupid but nice. You had to keep repeating yourself to Brian."

"What did you do down here?"

"I played Brian my songs." His face brightened. "I have an album to record soon."

Lately walked across the room. "Brian used to operate this thing." Lately flicked a switch back and forth on the mixing desk. "We made demos together."

"Is any of your stuff on those tapes?" Janney pointed at the reel-to-reel machines.

"No! Those tapes are gone." Johnny Lately gave a short laugh and looked at the floor. He slowly raised his head. Their eyes met. Both knew the truth.

"I saw you walk out of here the other night with that Derek mug. He was carrying boxes of tapes. Hear anything worth hearing?

"I heard you and Brian."

Lately became alert. "No! No, you didn't. Take that back. That's a lie. Do not start lying to me."

"No! I heard you alright. Just a few words. Right at the end of one of the tapes. The rest of the tape had been re-recorded over. You forgot to take one. Brian was playing the flute, you were listening, you spoke, you seemed to like it."

Lately stared at the wall above Janney's head. He was quiet for one or two minutes.

"They were my songs, my record, my words, my voice."

"Brian wrote the flute and piano pieces."

He suddenly shouted, "Who cares! They were my songs, I would have given him something, but he would not shut up about it. I was about to make an album. He could have played on it, but he kept arguing with me. The guy was an idiot—I just could not make him understand."

Lately became quiet again. He watched the floor. Janney knew it would be a bad idea to get his focus.

He stood upright, "So that's that then. They are going to do it to me again. I had a career once. People liked to see me onstage. Then in one day, all gone, debts, no work, no money. People laughed at me when I sat in pubs, girls ignored me, all because of those crooks at Range Records.

Lately's voice was choking. "It was all David Offen's fault. He put me in with them. Afterwards, he just didn't want to know. One day you're popular," there was a long pause. "I spent years painting buses."

"What about Brian?"

Lately suddenly shouted, his voice choking with tears, "What about him? It's not my fault he jumped."

Janney knew something was about to happen. When she was a child, she had seen the way dangerous people could behave.

She had seen that for some people, violence could come out of an impulse, especially when a bully faced someone helpless, with an idea no one would fight back.

Janey began putting all her energy into her arms. If he came at her, she would lift the small table and shove it into his face.

Mike and Malcolm discussed the telephone call from Hawkins. The spotlight seemed now to be off David. Mike said he would be a lot happier if he knew where Janney was and that she was safe. Malcolm remembered she said she would be stopping by the Back Door today.

"I have never been to this place. It's been a while since I went to a music pub. This Finlay Bruce seems like a character. Let's check it out and get you that lunch I promised."

Mike nodded. He wondered for a moment whether to call David but thought it could all wait. It was out of their hands and in the hands of the police now.

Malcolm drove to the Back Door. On the way, he asked Mike if they served food. Mike had no idea, but once he thought about it, the idea would have been ridiculous. The idea of eating with all that noise going on seemed funny.

Malcolm was about to suggest getting food first but maybe if Janney was there, they could all go off and eat together.

They entered the Back Door. Mike immediately saw Finlay Bruce at the bar. They walked over. Mike introduced Malcolm.

"Mr Offen, I have heard a great deal about you, all good."

"Please! Call me Malcolm. I have heard of you and of your wonderful establishment. You have given a few good bands their start here."

"If they did well, they did it for themselves. Still, it's nice if you can see the beginnings here. I have had a lot of rubbish play here as well. Please let me buy you both a drink."

Finlay called Tom over and was about to order a round of drinks. Malcolm mentioned he was driving. He just wanted a coffee if possible.

"A coffee, at the bar of a pub, of all places. Whatever next?" Finlay laughed, "Well, we are nothing if not cosmopolitan."

Mike casually mentioned, "Janney is on her way here."

"Yes!" said Finlay. I said I would be here at 2 pm. She should arrive soon."

Tom looked up from pouring the drinks, "Janney is downstairs in the studio. She has been down there an hour or so."

Mike began for the staircase. He did not run but he moved quickly. Malcolm followed. Finlay still stood at the bar; a bit surprised at the sudden departure. He followed once he saw them disappear.

Mike entered the studio. He saw Lately leaning over the table. Both Janney and Lately turned with surprise towards the door. It took Janney only a second more. She shoved the table back; Lately stumbled backwards, Janney stood up.

Mike said, "Janney, are you ok?" Malcolm appeared behind Mike. It took seconds to read the situation.

Suddenly Janney flew off her feet and at the face of Johnny Lately. He fell with his back on the floor. Janney jumped on top of his chest.

"You don't lay your hands on me," she screamed. She scratched at his face, then her fists punched straight into his nose and mouth. She felt his teeth move.

"You never touch me again! You never touch me," she screamed. She was losing control but also losing something she had carried around for years. She was not going to stop till it was all gone.

Malcolm and Mike watched the scene, but both could see it had to play itself out. Whatever was happening, it was important it played itself out.

Janney grabbed a heavy ashtray from the floor and lifted it up with both hands. She was going to bring its edge down on Johnny Lately's face, Mike raced forward and put his arm under Janney's waist and lifted her back up away from the bloodied man on the floor.

Janney released herself. She hissed at Mike to stay away. She was coming out from someplace deep within herself.

Mike stood in front of Janney and waited, Janney glared at Mike with wide eyes, then slowly she began to return.

Mike spoke softly. "You have hurt your fingers. You don't want to let them get bruised." Janney looked at him and then at her fingers in a daze.

"You need to get some cold water on them."

Mike put a gentle hand across her shoulders and guided her slowly to the door. Finlay appeared at the door, he stood aside for Mike and Janney.

Malcolm looked towards the door. "Finlay, could you call the police, please? I will stay here and watch over Mr Lately. Make sure nothing more happens to him."

# Chapter Thirty

David invited Malcolm, Mike and Janney to his house for a big breakfast on Saturday morning.

Seven days earlier David had been getting ready to prepare for his party that evening. David felt he lost any true sense of the time that had passed. He wondered how or if anyone had changed.

*'Perhaps they haven't. Perhaps only I have, maybe we are always changing,'* he wondered. *'Maybe we only bother to notice change when we want to, when it's obvious. Giving labels to the different changes that come, maybe to just satisfy ourselves, it's an easy option. Malcolm never seems to ever change, not since the war. He must have changed in some ways, but I can never see it.'* He knew Malcolm would never show all his cards.

Janney stood in the dining area looking at all the books stacked around the wall. She guessed David could not have read all these untouched shiny leather hardbacks. She would bet he had hardly opened them. No way would she ever want such a cluttered-up life. *'Why do rich people need to surround themselves with stuff'?*

Mike and Malcolm sat at the dinner table waiting for David to come in with the breakfast. The newspapers were full of election trivia.

They both discussed America's growing involvement in what could become a long-term war. They hoped the UK would stay well out. *'Nothing to win, no way to win it'* was Malcolm's assessment.

David eventually entered with a large tray of tea, coffee and toast. He had staff that would follow in later with the breakfast food. Everyone sat down around the table.

They had gathered that morning because the night before, Inspector Hawkins had dropped by. He invited David over to the station, "Come along midday" Johnny Lately had been charged and he was in the cells.

David noticed Mike and Janney were getting close. He was no master of body language, but it didn't take much to see they were comfortable in each other's space. Mike was looking down at a newspaper open across the table, Janney stood behind him, she leaned forward and rested her head onto his shoulder, *'Well,'* thought David, *'so it goes.'*

Malcolm told David that business could still proceed but there would need to be a cooling-off period. They would need to reinvent David's business a little, rebuild the image. Malcolm said it did not have to be a bad thing. In a way, it had all been inevitable. Nothing lasts, everything changes.

There were now so many new sharks in the water, it was no longer possible to play the same game, the same way. How can you know who you might be dealing with?

Malcolm poured some tea, "What exactly did Hawkins say, David?"

"Just come over midday. He will bring me up to date. No more really than that. Lately has been charged. Wait till we get there. I said I would bring you guys."

David poured the milk, "I have called three papers, no exclusives. I will see them this evening, give them what little I know. It should be in the Sunday or Monday editions."

Mike got David's attention, "Tell Hawkins you intend to do that, say it to him in front of us, say that everything the inspector tells you will be repeated. If he oversteps the mark, that becomes his lookout." David just nodded his head, a part of him was tired of Mike's advice, it seemed now it always came with a price tag on his patience.

Mike kept at it. "Make sure you do not overstep the mark with the papers either. They will try to manoeuvre you. Every word out of your mouth is worth money to them."

"Thanks, Mike, I will be careful. This is not my first time on the Ferris Wheel. This must seem like a strange one for you Mike, the police are on our side."

Malcolm saw things were getting a little off topic. "There are times to trust the police, there are policemen to trust. I would give Bill a little latitude if I were you, he is working for our interests."

Janney thought the room had a strange atmosphere, but then again, what could you compare the situation to?

The conversation turned to normal things. Always a great habit, disappear away from your thoughts, while at the same time, still offer your opinions in normal conversations.

Once breakfast was over, the four got into David's car and drove to the station. The journey was quiet. Everyone listened to the news on the radio. It seemed more relevant now that everyone was sharing it.

They entered the station, gave their name and asked for Inspector Hawkins. He appeared and brought them once again to the interview room. The table was covered with papers and photographs. He had two extra chairs brought in. He pulled a chair out for Janney; she wasn't sure where to look, he was a policeman after all.

"Thanks for coming, everyone," said the inspector.

"Thanks for inviting us," said David. There followed several seconds of silence.

"Where are we, Bill?" Malcolm asked.

"We have a confession of sorts. It's having to be dragged out of him. I think with the state he was in; he is now enjoying a chance to relax, the chance to talk. We have to be careful, with what we ask, what with all the pills that might still be working through his system. He wants to know when we are going to bring charges against you, Miss Malone."

Janney looked back in her mind to all the excuses she heard as a child, one to cover all eventualities.

"I was defending myself."

"Yes, Miss Malone, that is what I thought. You can bring charges yourself if you wish. In any case, I will need a more complete statement from you, at your convenience. It's uncertain what he intends to plead guilty to at the trial."

"You think he might not?" Mike said.

"He only enters the real world for short visits. His lawyer is being very helpful. He is trying to persuade Mr Lately to admit what can be proven. Some denials look stupid, at least to a jury. In a roundabout way, admitting to nothing can suit our purpose."

The Inspector stopped short. "Sorry! I should not have said that. We are not prosecutors, we only arrest people."

The Inspector began organising the papers on the desk. "I must make a distinction here, of all which we might prove with the evidence we have, coupled with those offences he has admitted. We must continue to examine those offences he has not admitted to, those which remain to be proven."

"These are the offences and charges the Crown Prosecution Service still must decide whether to bring. That will rely on whether there is sufficient evidence to show guilt at a trial if they are not admitted."

The Inspector settled his attention on the group. "Here is what we know happened," Inspector Hawkins began the story from before Christmas.

"Johnny Lately had been invited to release a single, on the back of a renewed interest in his career following a television advertisement using an old song of his. He wrote several new songs and went to the Back Door to make demonstration recordings. He met Brian Nicholls there who helped him record the songs. Lately allowed Mr Nicholls to play on the demo recordings and saw he was dramatically improving his songs by adding flute and piano. Mr Nicholls also wrote down the music arrangements for the flute and piano."

The inspector paused for questions. There were none. "Lately burglarised Brian Nicholls' flat, stole all the arrangements and any tapes Mr Nicholls had there. He stole from the studio what he thought were all the tape recordings he and Brian Nicholls made at the Back Door. Miss Malone found one that Lately missed. We entered Mr Lately's flat. We have all the material he stole. He has admitted to the burglary."

The Inspector waited again for questions. "He has some trouble admitting that Mr Nicholls contributed anything to the single he recorded. The written arrangements have all of Mr Nicholls' fingerprints and handwriting. He brought the written arrangements he stole to the studio and made his record."

Once again, the Inspector stopped. "This is where we might need to persuade a jury. Once the single was released, Mr Nicholls heard the record and realised what had happened. Lately knew that Mr Nicholls was attending the party to speak to you, Malcolm. Once Mr Nicholls arrived, Lately intercepted him at the door and invited him upstairs for a chat."

"Mr Lately initially denied he ever went to the attic with Mr Nicholls. Mr Lately finally admitted he was upstairs in the attic at some point but not necessarily at the same time as Mr Nicholls. His lawyer helped us with that. Lately's shoe print got us that far. We believe Lately came to the party to stop Mr Nicholls speaking with you Malcolm. It may also be the case that he was also paid by parties unknown to sabotage the party and the guests with LSD."

The Inspector directed his attention specifically to David, "Mr Offen. If it is the case that he was acting for others, he may believe they will help him, either now or in the future. If so, he will eventually realise that is not going to happen. We are hoping Mr Lately will then provide a bit more information."

# Chapter Thirty-One

The room became silent as everyone sought the other's face. Although the facts as they were explained were clear, it was also clear that there existed a lot of room to create and spread doubt as to guilt or responsibility.

Mike broke the silence. "What is your assessment Inspector, how far will the Prosecution Service go with this." Inspector Hawkins raised both hands with palms facing each other "Somebody attended the party with a bag of LSD tablets. We believe he or she gave Mr Nicholls a drink with a substantial amount of LSD. The likely room where this occurred was the attic. Inside the attic, for an hour or so, Mr Nicholls consumed or was forced to consume a great deal of LSD."

This time the Inspector directed his attention to Malcolm. "We believe that the purpose of the LSD was to destroy Mr Nicholls' credibility or indeed ability to talk to you, to make accusations or to give you any information. That amount of LSD, very strong LSD I might add, might well have caused long-term harm to Mr Nicholls' mental wellbeing. It is extremely unlikely that anybody would willingly consume the amount of LSD Mr Nicholls had in his system."

The Inspector spoke with a new emphasis. "LSD also holds a small amount of strychnine in its composition. The amount consumed by Mr Nicholls might even have become lethal."

The room became silent at this information, the Inspector continued. "There was a lot of dust in the attic, more dropping every minute because of the music vibrations. The windows were opened, maybe to allow air in the room. Lately will not assist us as to when he entered or left the attic. He refuses to say how long he was downstairs before Mr Nicholls fell. He admits he saw him fall and said that is when he left. We have a couple of statements which say Mr Lately appeared in the garden area for the first time just before Mr Nicholls fell. It is clear from several eyewitness accounts Mr Lately had a great deal of dust about him.

"Mr Nicholls would have suffered delusions sitting in the chair facing the window. It may be suggested he left the chair and walked through the window to watch the moon. There was a full moon that night, which could be seen from the centre of the open window. Just before the fall, someone already placed a great amount of LSD in the punch bowl and into several glasses resting on the tables."

Inspector Hawkins turned his attention specifically to David, "Lately has a very deep hatred towards you, Mr Offen. He blames you for much of what has occurred in his life. He very much wishes you harm. Lately takes some delight with the idea of your guests suddenly hallucinating, all against their will, becoming frightened, calling for help, with you not knowing what was going on. He hoped the whole thing would destroy your reputation, make you a lot of enemies, lose you a great deal of business."

"He very much hoped you would drink the punch yourself. He wanted to torment you if he caught you under its influence. Mr Lately admits he immediately left the house after the fall. The fall had surprised him, maybe shocked him. My own thought is that the fall was not intended, not planned, in fact, the fall itself probably prevented more guests from becoming intoxicated other than the three young girls. I believe Mr Nicolls fall and death caused Mr Lately to panic, and he ran away from the house."

Inspector Hawkins turned his attention to Janney, "During our interview, you mentioned how some people walked to the gate immediately following the fall. I kept running the scenario in my head. That's when an idea hit me."

Inspector Hawkins picked up several photographs from the table. "A lot of pictures were taken that evening. Many appeared in the newspapers. Many were taken to the newspapers by photographers with the hope of selling them. Many were kept by the papers but not all were used. Please look at these and tell me what appears to you."

The photos were handed back and forth. They could see Lately leaving through the gates. His black oily hair was covered and caked in a lot of heavy dust. One picture revealed his back. His sky-blue coat had thick grey dust across his shoulders.

"I remember you brushing off dust when you left the attic, that was only after a few moments," said Malcolm.

"I should have at least put that piece together then," said the inspector. "I had not considered it meant anything if a few guests had slipped away before the police arrived. I still had their names if I wanted to interview them. Well! Live and learn."

"Mr Lately will not admit to manslaughter. He thinks his lack of intention and his presence downstairs saves him from responsibility. He still insists at this point that Mr Nicholls did it to himself.

"He will not admit to possession of LSD. It's clear someone brought a lot of LSD to the party. Mr Lately is the only suspect we have on that issue. Except there remains the question, where did he obtain such a quantity? It's possible he obtained it by himself. I am of the view that he was approached. There is a view that a third party thought your reputation and indeed your business could be harmed if several people suffered harmful hallucinations at your party, especially if it were against their will. I can say with some certainty that Mr Lately would have enjoyed that outcome. He even laughed at the idea.

"In some respects, you have been very lucky Mr Offen, I have seen instances where people have had their reputations ruined, their lives ruined, when actually innocent, of any wrongdoing."

David hardly knew what to say. "You don't seem to have a lot of faith in the law or your police force inspector."

"If I cross a one-way street, I look both ways, that is the extent of my faith in others Mr Offen. I have a lot of faith in a lot of things, but generally, not people. I keep my faith for myself. I can then live with the blame I get from others."

"My apologies, Mr Offen, sitting in an interview room, I get tempted to be cute with people. If you put all your faith in something, it becomes harder to look at it realistically. A policeman spends a great deal of his time just trying to get on with his life."

"Mr Lately's lawyer is trying to convince him that an admission here and there now will serve him better than demanding everything from a jury. Some honesty grants credibility. More confusion for the jury. As things stand, the possible charges are Manslaughter, certainly GBH upon Mr Nicholls as well as upon your guests, Assault and Imprisonment upon you Miss Malone, it's all on the table. The CPS will make their decision soon, the coroner's hearing has been postponed."

Everyone was silent for a moment. Janney spoke first, "I should have smashed his face in."

David stood and offered the inspector his hand. "Thank you. Inspector, thank you for everything you have done. We all owe you a debt."

Malcolm shook his friend's hand. "You are doing a great job here, Bill. I wish I could say more right now, but let's catch up again soon."

The four looked at each other. It seemed more should be said. They all felt there were questions that could be asked but any questions would be just for questions' sake. They each wanted to get out of the police station.

Once they left the station, Mike took the initiative and pointed at the pub across the road. At first, David was reluctant but then Malcolm spoke with some certainty, "Listen to him, let's go." They followed orders and walked across the road.

Once they entered, got their drinks and sat, they could feel each other relax. "This is a nice pub," said Janney. David and Mike looked at each other and smiled.

"I am going to hold all of Lately's payments from the single," said Malcolm. "Let any lawyers work out the right and wrong of it. Tell the papers that, Dave."

David nodded. Mike told David to hold off on any statement concerning LSD in the punch bowl. The papers will get a better story anyway once Lately appears in the Magistrate Court. Lately might even admit to more in the next few days.

Mike sat there but he did not feel like a lawyer. He did feel Janney lean on his arm as he spoke, "You tell the papers of how Brian had his part of the record stolen and you will have them on your side all the way. Just promise you will give more when you can."

"Mr Public Relations," said David.

"Any idea where you're going now, Dave?" Malcolm said.

"Yes! I thought of it all last night. I am going to downsize, I am going to sell the house, all my junk."

Everyone seemed surprised. "I have been listening to Mike, the house has bad karma, dharma, or farma or something. In any case, I do not want to walk around the place anymore, bad vibes. I need to get my head straight, need a holiday."

Janney was enjoying feeling part of the team. "What are you going to do?"

"I was thinking about property development. Do something positive, take a broken-down property, fix it up, sell it. Once I am up and running, know what I am doing, the right way to do it, I might buy a property, turn it into a first-rate music palace, who knows. Have you any suggestions, Mike?"

"Make sure it has a quiet room, where you can drink in peace. Get some good peanuts in," said Mike.

David felt a little more at peace than he had felt since before the party. He knew inside he felt better than for a long time. "I need to step back and see who the new players are now. I can't work with people who had any part in what happened, you lie down with dogs, you get up with flies."

Malcolm smiled his broadest smile, "That's the family spirit, David. I think the property angle is a great idea. I would be happy to come in on a few deals."

A few days later, Johnny Lately pleaded guilty in the Magistrate Court for false imprisonment of Janney, as well as the burglary of Brian Nicholls flat, but not guilty to any of the other charges made against him. The matter was forwarded to the Crown Court for trial.

At trial, he pleaded not guilty to putting LSD in the punch bowl. He said he believed in the positive benefits of LSD, but he would never impose it on others. Brian believed the same. They both had respect for the rights of everyone to make their own decisions.

Lately insisted Brian had brought his own LSD to the party. Brian took all his LSD by himself.

The defence tried to argue that persons unknown placed LSD in the punch bowl. Lately claimed he had not imagined for a moment Brian Nicholls would take so much of the drug by himself, alone by himself, then take his own life. He worried about his friend and warned him many times to be careful. He had tried to help his friend with his drug problem. He left his friend alone, seemingly asleep in the attic and then saw the fall from downstairs. He was in deep shock once it happened, he remembered little.

He was about to make Brian and himself famous together. He would have given him full credit for all contributions on the new album.

He talked at length about their collaboration, of his repeatedly offering his friend help with his drug problem. Had he imagined what Brian would do, he would have stopped him. It was tragic. They were close friends and had a great future together.

Mike and Janney attended the trial. They watched the arguments and the search by the defence for uncertainty within any testimony, anything a jury member or two might decide was important, unclear, in dispute or what they may personally define as *'reasonable doubt'*.

Janney gave her evidence. When challenged, she appeared small in the witness box. The accusations that she attacked and beat up Lately appeared ridiculous. She had been in fear for her life. She was defending herself just as Mike and Malcolm opened the door to the studio to save her.

She gave the court full details of all that was said while held against her will, trapped in the studio.

She watched Lately as he watched her. She wanted a chance to talk to Lately, ask who was fearful now.

Lately's arrival at the party, then his long absence, his appearance at the party just before the fall and then leaving immediately afterwards, covered in cakes of heavy dust from the attic, it all challenged his credibility.

The fact he presented Brian Nicholls' music arrangements as his own, as well as the tapes hidden within his apartment all compounded his clear deceit.

Despite his denials, he was found guilty of all charges.